PERFECT

WORLD

PERFECT

WORLD

IAN COLFORD   A NOVEL

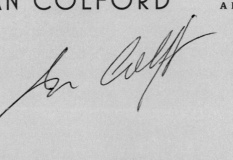

Freehand Books gratefully acknowledges the support of the Canada Council for the Arts for its publishing program. ¶ Freehand Books acknowledges the financial support for its publishing program provided by the Government of Canada through the Canada Book Fund.

 Canada Council Conseil des Arts   Alberta
for the Arts   du Canada   Government

Freehand Books
515 – 815 1st Street SW Calgary, Alberta T2P 1N3
www.freehand-books.com

Book orders: LitDistCo
100 Armstrong Avenue Georgetown, Ontario L7G 5S4
Telephone: 1-800-591-6250 Fax: 1-800-591-6251
orders@litdistco.ca
www.litdistco.ca

Library and Archives Canada Cataloguing in Publication

Colford, Ian, author
Perfect world / Ian Colford.

Issued also in electronic format.
ISBN 978-1-55481-286-8 (paperback).
ISBN 978-1-4604-0563-5 (html).
ISBN 978-1-77048-604-1 (pdf)

I. Title.

PS8555.O44P47 2016   C813'.54   C2015-908606-X   C2015-908607-8

Edited by Barbara Scott
Book design by Natalie Olsen, Kisscut Design
Author photo by Hilary Lynd
Printed on FSC® recycled paper and bound in Canada by Marquis Book Printing

To anyone whose life has been
altered by mental illness

At human pace I see

spun from the flattened centre

the white scut blown as thistledown

and gleaming jewel-bright, upturned

to the blind indifferent world,

a single eye.

PHOEBE HESKETH

ONE

TOM BRACKETT IS standing outside, waiting for his father to return home from work. Tom's habit is to wait in the driveway, even on days like today when it is very cold. He wipes his nose on the sleeve of his jacket, kicks gravel with his foot, breathes steam into the air. He looks at the sky. Black birds scream and taunt as they circle overhead.

His mother is in the house with his baby sister. When he got home from school, he crept inside and deposited his book bag in his room. Then he left the house quietly, by the side door. Lately, his mother has been having "spells." This is what his father calls them, and when he repeats the word to himself, savouring its brevity and strangeness — its suggestion of magic — he tries to take comfort from the way it hints at something of short duration. There is, however, an expression in his father's eyes when he speaks of his mother that Tom doesn't like, that he wants to challenge and wipe out — a mournful, canine acceptance of yet one more thing that is beyond comprehension. But Tom is smart enough to recognize that there are boundaries he must observe. He tries to stay out of the way when he can. He enters the house with the practised stealth of a burglar, alert to the starkly negative potential of his mother's presence.

Through layers of grey cloud and a tangled grid of branches, the day's light is beginning to fade. The trees are losing their leaves and the air is dense and moist. Sometimes his mind drifts and he considers nature — all the mysteries there are in the world, all the things he doesn't understand and has still to learn — and is both stymied and excited by the thought. He has looked at maps, but he can never work out the distances. All he knows is that Paris, Cairo, and Athens are beyond his ken. But there is no hurry. He has time. He looks up. The approaching snowfall seems to hover just out of reach, an invisible burden weighing down the early November air. No one is around, the birds are gone and Tom hears only the slow rustle of dying leaves as a breeze passes overhead, and, occasionally, the slick whisper of car tires.

The community is called Black River and consists of fifty or so families and half a dozen churches scattered along a desolate stretch of highway. The Brackett house is set well back from the road; the driveway snakes a hundred feet through trees. The nearest neighbour's house — the Joffreys' — is visible a short distance off through scrubby brush and sparse wood-land, but might as well be miles away for all the contact that takes place between the two families. The daughter, Hallie, is in his class at school, and he can remember a time when his parents and the Joffreys exchanged visits almost every other week. But then his mother had the baby and things got strange, and the visiting ended.

Tom waits midway between house and highway, where he can keep both within sight. After a few minutes he hears the familiar chug and rumble of his father's pickup. It pulls in at the mouth of the driveway and Tom, anxious but unwilling to let his father see his anxiety, saunters down to meet it.

"Hi," he says as he gets in and slams the door. He doesn't look at his father.

Charles Brackett gestures in the direction of the house.

"Any action up there?"

"I didn't see nothing," Tom answers. He flips his hair back from his eyes. He is thirteen and vaguely resentful of his father's apparent indifference to the sudden changes that have swooped down on his life and stripped it of predictability and routine. His confusion is real, but he can't find words to express it. A niggling voice whispers in his ear a warning to keep his questions to himself. His father has offered no explanation. This is the man who always knows what to do, who can fix whatever's broken. To get through the day Tom must ignore his fears and follow his father's lead, staying quiet in the expectation that the situation will right itself on its own. He won't accept that his faith has been shaken. All recent evidence to the contrary, he refuses to see that his father has become a foreigner in his own life, wearing the awestruck expression of someone for whom everything is new and terrifying.

As he reverses the truck into the road, Tom's father says firmly, "Buckle up, buster," and Tom does what he's told.

They cover five miles in silence.

"Bad day at school?" his father ventures.

"It was okay."

"You just let me know, any of those teachers give you a hard time."

Tom shifts in his seat. He's heard this offer before but doesn't understand what it means. None of his teachers have ever been less than civil to him. He's liked some better than others, but he's never been intimidated, bullied, or victimized. He has never regarded his treatment as unfair. When he fails a test, it's always his own fault. His classmates are little cause for concern. He supposes that he is neither liked nor disliked, but doesn't think about it much. He moves freely, from one group to another. People don't seek him out, but neither do they shun him. At least once each day he experiences the smile of a person he doesn't know. On the continuum from most to least popular, he finds himself squarely in the middle, a position that suits him very well.

"You just let me know," his father repeats, nodding for emphasis. "Any of those fuckers give you a hard time they'll have me to answer to."

"Whatever," Tom mutters, and turns his gaze to the window.

They pass miles of bush and forest and abandoned farmland before the first houses appear, thin-walled structures pitched to alarming angles by the slowly and unevenly receding clay upon which their foundations were built. Uninterested, Tom watches them drift by. The houses are empty and there are no people in sight.

Before Tom left his own house this morning his mother locked herself in the bathroom with his baby sister, Beverly. Standing outside the door, he heard the sounds of splashing and the hushed chatter of a one-sided conversation. His mother was bathing the baby. She would be naked while doing this. He knew she would be naked because twice now he has walked into the bathroom while she was giving Beverly a bath. The door was open and he heard nothing until it was too late and he was looking at his mother, kneeling in the tub in two inches of water and using a soapy cloth to wipe the baby's tiny body. She didn't acknowledge him, didn't pause or alter the cooing, singsong tone of her voice. Her breasts dangled above the baby's head, strangely weighted, like plastic bags filled with water. The cleft of hair at the base of her belly struck him like a gentle rebuke. Since the last of these accidental intrusions his mother has been closing and locking the bathroom door. Bathing the baby has become an obsession. How dirty can a baby get? And it seems to him there are other things she should be doing, like buying fresh milk and making a lunch for him to take to school. Without her deft touch the house is in a state of chaos. Dirty laundry has piled up. He's wearing the same underwear as yesterday. What should he do? This morning he stood at the bathroom door and listened for a moment, thinking maybe she would finish soon so he could use the toilet. But he gave up when he realized he was going to be late for school and instead went into the woods where he pissed behind a rock and watched the steam from his urine rise into the frigid morning air.

In a few minutes they reach New Minas. His father pulls the truck into the lot of the McDonald's. Simultaneously, without a word — as if with the rehearsed precision of trapeze artists — they climb out of the truck. Their doors slam in unison. Crossing the lot, Tom is at pains to keep up with his father's long, loping stride. In the restaurant Tom orders a Big Mac with fries and a chocolate milkshake. His father orders a chicken burger, large fries, onion rings, and, after a thoughtful pause, a coffee.

They wait for their food. Tom's father is not old, yet he behaves in an elderly manner: waiting for his order, he retreats to the back, away from the counter, his hands folded in front of him, his posture slightly stooped as if he were leaning on a cane. His father is not the kind of man who raises his voice. He will retreat first and attack later. His anger, when it comes, results from frustration and seethes rather than explodes. He swears, bangs his fist on the table, slams the door on the way out. Normally, though, his temper is so even and placid that Tom sometimes imagines him as a cow: imperturbable, living a rudimentary life. His father is always grubby — grime under his father's fingernails is one of Tom's earliest memories, along with a mingled stench of sweat, tobacco, and dirt: the smell of an honest day's work. Overalls, scarred work boots, a soiled cap proclaiming "Joe's Garage." Tom isn't sure how to feel about this. Should he admire his father's honest, plodding ways? Should he ridicule them, hold the man in contempt? For Tom the answers to these questions change from one moment to the next. Sometimes he wishes that one thing in his life could be simple and obvious.

They collect their orders and take a table at the front of the restaurant, beside the row of windows. Outside, it is nearly dark. All the cars and trucks have their lights on and the beams spill eerily along the road. The shutting down of another day. Tom remembers the homework waiting for him — a list of questions for his Canadian Studies course and a mathematics quiz — both due tomorrow. But it's nothing serious. He can take care of it in less than an hour if he puts his mind to it.

Normally they eat in complete silence, shovelling in their food with the unblinking efficiency of the truly famished. Tonight his father says, "Snow," and when Tom glances up, his father gestures with an onion ring.

At the sight of the huge flakes slanting downward Tom feels a surge of warmth, the same one that gets his blood moving every year at the onset of winter, a weightless, wafting sensation that almost makes him think he could float on air. Snow has always meant hockey, tobogganing, a fire in the fireplace, his mother's hot chocolate made in a big pot on the stove, stirred with a wooden spoon. For years now, about a week before Christmas, he and his father have ventured into the woods and cut down a tree. His mother had final approval, but only once in all those years did she send them back out to find another. Will things be different this year? Is there anything left that he can count on?

"Dad?"

Charles Brackett raises an eyebrow but keeps his gaze on the snow outside.

"Mmmm?"

"How long is Mom going to be...you know, like she is? Sort of...." Tom's question trails off as he gropes for a word that ultimately eludes his grasp. He shifts in his seat.

Charles looks at his son.

"She's turned a bit odd on us, hasn't she Tom."

His father seems for a moment to smile, possibly at the understated irony of his comment, but the smile fades quickly and beneath the pitiless restaurant lights, wrinkles and crevices appear on his face that Tom's never noticed before. His father grows older as he looks on — ten, twenty years. His coarse skin acquires the puffy, unwholesome pallor of the sleep deprived; his cheeks sink upon themselves like flattened cushions. Charles Brackett says nothing further because there is, apparently, nothing to say. Tom's confusion deepens. Years later he will realize that his father had no answer, that it was unfair to expect one, that Charles Brackett could not possibly have known that this was the last time he would eat at McDonald's with his son.

Today, though, the silence seems like withholding.

So Tom is left alone with his thoughts and fears. Within the week he will be moved to his grandmother's house outside Liverpool, down on the South Shore. A few years after that his father will move to Halifax and Tom will have no idea if his mother and sister went with him. Tom will stay with his grandmother in her dusty, cluttered house near the ocean until he is nineteen. He will see little of his father and nothing of his mother and sister. While he will miss his home and his family, he will not miss his mother's peculiar ways or the churning and the tightness in his stomach, the not knowing when the next strange or awful thing will happen. To be sure, he will be shaken by the sadness of it, by nagging questions and dreams that will recur with disturbing clarity, bringing with them a memory of his mother naked, the murmuring singsong of her voice and its undecipherable message. But eventually he will be happy, after a fashion, and will pass without further scars through adolescence, drifting amiably toward adulthood with a calmly acquiescent temperament so uncommon to youth that it will appear, to some, like apathy or coldness.

TWO

EVEN WITH THE PILLOW over his head Tom can't sleep. It doesn't seem to matter the hour of the day or night, Halifax is crowded and noisy: endlessly bustling with the clamour of traffic and voices, enveloping him with smells — fried food, vehicle exhaust, the harbour water with its pervasive odour of salt and decay — that blend in his nostrils with an exotic savouriness. Sitting at the window of his tiny top-floor room in the Hollis Street Hotel, he enjoys an unobstructed view over the roofs of buildings all the way down to the water, and beyond that to Dartmouth, on the other side of the harbour. "The deepest natural harbour in the world." This is what his grade-eleven history teacher Mr. Winger told the class, and for some reason the fact struck Tom as interesting. He also read in a book that "George's Island arches out of the water like a woman's breast," which he realized was not a fact but a matter of opinion, but which he also found interesting and now, he is glad to finally discover that it's an opinion with which he can agree.

This is not all new to him. He's taken the bus up to Halifax before, initially to look for work, but more recently just to hang out with friends, hear live music, and visit the newest pub and eat greasy food. Alfie Tucker, Shirley Monroe, Susan Wood, Barry Leppard. All of them are living here and paying their way, working in restaurants or for landscaping or house-painting companies. Minimum-wage jobs. Usually when he visits he sleeps on someone's floor, saving his money for movies and beer and cigarettes. But this time he's come for a different reason and has taken a room — the cheapest he could find — in order to give himself a private retreat. He's going to see his mother today. His sister Beverly will be there too. He hasn't seen her since she was two months old.

Ten days ago, when his father called him at work, Tom had to keep him waiting because he was changing someone's oil. He started working at the Shell station near exit 20 on Highway 103 when he was seventeen and he's been pumping gas ever since. Pretty soon he'll be able to afford a second-hand car.

"Hello? Dad?" Tom had to yell above the roar of a car's engine.

"Tom, you want to see your mother?"

"What? What's going on?"

"You want to see your mother or not?"

Tom wiped his free hand on his coveralls. What was his father doing, calling him out of nowhere like this, sounding slightly drunk, pressing him to deliver an immediate decision as if this would be the last chance he would ever have?

"Dad, what's going on?"

"It's up to you, Tom. I can get you in to see her. Just you say the word."

"'Get me in to see her?' What is she, in the hospital or something? Is she sick?"

The line stayed quiet, though Tom could still hear the jagged rasp of his father's breathing.

"Dad?"

His father didn't speak.

Tom sighed. "Why don't you just tell me where she is and I'll go see her myself?"

"Can't do it, Tom. Can't do it. I'll set it up though. I'll go with you. I know you're a busy man. When do you think you can get up here?"

They decided on a week Tuesday. Last night Tom took the bus into town. At eleven o'clock he is to meet his father outside the Tim Horton's in the Scotia Square mall.

THOUGH IT'S JUST AFTER six a.m., Tom gets dressed and goes downstairs. He exchanges a nod with the bored young man at the desk and slips out the door. Parked cars line the street, but there's no one else around. He's not used to having nothing to do and nowhere to be. The sense of aimlessness is not unpleasant, but he doesn't know what to do with it. Instead of feeling free, he feels irresponsible, like he's shirking some duty, and for a while, as he walks, he struggles with senseless guilt.

The September morning is cool. The air drifting in off the water carries with it a suggestion of sea spray mixed with premonitions of autumn. Most of Tom's walking is done on bare earth, and in the city he always notices how the concrete sidewalk stubbornly resists his step, seems in some obscure way to hamper his movements. He wants speed in his life, craves change, and there is a maddening sameness to his days — at the gas station, at his grandmother's house — that occasionally makes him want to smash something or, more often, fills him with an urge to run off to some far-flung corner of the earth where he knows nobody and nobody knows him, and then keep going, just to see what he can see.

At thirteen, when he realized that he wasn't just visiting his grandmother, that he was going to be living with her, he pouted and cried, uselessly, like a child, and hated himself for it. He was given a small upstairs bedroom with an ancient black-and-white television and some books and magazines — and his father sent his things over from the other house — but it wasn't home and never would be. What hurt the most was being dumped like an unwanted pet. He passed the first days in resentful silence, only coming out of his room for meals. At night he dreamed it was all a mistake, that his father came to get him and they drove home and everything went back to the way it had been before the baby was born. But weeks passed and the dreams faded, and from his grandmother's bewilderment at his presence he realized that this new living arrangement was just as much a surprise to her. She sat at the kitchen table doing puzzles, smiling when he came into the room, but it was obvious that she had no idea what to do with him. For months he suffered moments of crushing sadness, as close to despair as he ever hoped to come. He looked for ways to amuse himself, but the search was often fruitless and over the years he lost count of the number of sluggish Saturday afternoons he spent staring through a window at a day that seemed to last forever, the time passing with all the vigour of a slow drip from a faucet. The house, situated far from town at the edge of a swampy field overrun with cattails and soggy yellow grass, as grey and weathered as his mood, was a constant reminder to Tom that there was nothing right about a teenage boy having to live with his seventy-year-old grandmother.

Tom's grandfather had died before Tom was born, and his grandmother had grown eccentric in her solitude. There were times when she seemed to forget about him. More than once he surprised her in the kitchen in her underwear. Sometimes she fixed dinner for herself but not for him. The place was filled with dust and useless objects that hadn't budged for decades. It reeked of mildew and trapped air. His grandmother smoked and drank, though always behind the closed door of her own room and only at night. He couldn't help but smell the booze on her in the morning when, with her hands trembling, she burnt the porridge or spilled the orange juice, and see it in the slow foggy focus of her eyes, her stuttering movements and alarming intervals of confusion, when she called him Charlie or even Sam, her dead husband's name. Back then they'd laughed it off, amused by her lapses. Lately, though, she's been making the mistake more often, and there's nothing funny about it.

He can't remember exactly when or how he found out that his grandmother was subsisting on a miserly government pension and that his father was sending money every month, not just to cover Tom's food and clothes and school supplies, but to keep her alive. She must have let something slip, or maybe told him outright. Whatever the case, in his memory one day he simply knew it for a fact. On Tom's birthday, as predictable as the birds in spring, his father would show up at the door with an armload of badly wrapped parcels and some groceries in a plastic bag, looking more stooped and haggard with each passing year. The first couple of times Charles Brackett's silent company was a comfort. He stayed for a few days, making repairs around the house, painting whatever needed it, saying almost nothing but occasionally bestowing a smile on his desperate son. Tom followed him around, holding the ladder, fetching tools, helping to mix or stir the paint, hoping that this shy camaraderie would lead to something more. But always in the end his father disappeared as abruptly as he'd arrived, gone one morning without a word of warning or goodbye. In later years, when the silences took on a surly overtone and Tom was old enough to recognize a drunk when he saw one, he made sure to be elsewhere as the old man went about his work and was glad when the visit was over and his father was gone. In between the visits from his father he heard nothing from his family, and with the passage of time he didn't even bother wondering what might be going on. The loneliness persisted, but as he settled deeper into this new life with his grandmother, his old life receded until the distances were too vast to cross without great effort, and he left it behind, shelved like some project to which he planned, someday, to return.

HE BUYS A CUP of coffee and a bagel at Perks on the water-front, then heads back to the hotel, following Water Street where he can keep the rising sun in his sights. The morning is beginning to warm up and the sky is high with a smudge of florid pink at the horizon. His father's refusal to tell him where his mother is awakens him once more to the realization that he's been kept in the dark by both his grandmother and his father. Whenever he mentioned his mother and sister to his grandmother, she either pretended not to hear or went to her room. When he asked his father, the response — if one was forthcoming — was, "You just worry about yourself, Tom. Let me worry about them." He assumes the house where he grew up has been sold, though nobody ever troubled to tell him. But once, a few years ago — on an evening when his grandmother started drinking earlier than usual and by nine o'clock was snoring behind the door of her room — lonely and tearful he dialled his old number. "Sorry sonny," the woman who answered said. "Never heard of a Charles Brackett." Then, her composure almost dissolving when he sobbed into the phone, "Are you sure you've got the right number?" Ashamed, he hung up and choked back the tears. At the time he felt orphaned, but enough time has passed now that the old house holds little meaning for him. It's difficult to conjure the details of its blueprint and he can't be sure if the images that come to mind are the product of memory or imagination.

At the hotel he switches on the television and watches a newscast and then a repeat of the same newscast, but still arrives at the Scotia Square mall well ahead of time. Growing anxious now, wondering what the day holds in store, he spends the spare minutes lingering about the shops, loitering next to displays of merchandise that don't interest him, fleeing from eager or mistrustful sales clerks. He walks back and forth past the Tim Horton's at the base of the escalator, but with thirty minutes to kill retreats to the drug store. He buys a newspaper and wanders over to the food court. None of the food appeals to him but he buys another bagel and coffee anyway. Taking a seat at a table in the back against the wall, where he hopes his presence will go unnoticed, he reads sordid and depressing accounts of a ten-year-old boy who killed his puppy with a BB gun, and a man who was secretly married to three women at the same time.

The possibility of arriving at the rendezvous ahead of his father is making him lightheaded. His ears ring and he breaks into a sweat. Why does he not want to be waiting when Charles trudges along looking for him? What is to be gained from being late? And he realizes, with the intuition of someone who has been blindsided too many times and left to figure things out for himself, that if he can catch a glimpse of his father without being seen, he might be better prepared for whatever surprise the old man is waiting to spring on him.

So he waits.

When he approaches the Tim Horton's shortly after eleven, the sight of his father engaged in conversation with a young woman at first startles him, and then fills him with an inexplicable sadness, as if he's just received the bad news he's been expecting. He does not notice their fingers linked across the table until he's close enough to be seen, and then it's too late. He has to go through with this.

His father stands.

In the eight months since Tom's last birthday Charles Brackett has changed, and not for the better. He's lost some flesh, but it's more than that. Tom is hardly prepared for a man who looks shrunken and derelict, wizened and uncared for like something left outside for too long, exposed to the elements. His breath catches in his throat. In his memory his father is wiry but strong, maybe not always at the top of his game but at least capable of putting on a show. Today the flesh at his neck is hanging loose and his jeans droop baggily at the crotch. He is missing a front tooth, and the whites of his eyes are cross-hatched with tiny veins. His father extends his hand. There's nothing else for Tom to do but grip it. However, the vice-like embrace that follows takes him completely by surprise.

"Tom, my boy! Can't tell you how glad I am to see you! Christ, how are you?"

They perform a brief shuffle among the coffee shop seats until Tom manages to regain his balance and loosen his father's grip. People are watching.

"Hey, Dad," he says. He smiles. "You're looking good."

The young woman is standing close behind his father.

"Tom, this is Crystal."

She steps forward and they shake hands. Her hand is soft and feels small and childish in his, though her nails are shapely and painted red. Tom guesses she might be twenty-five, though it's difficult to see what she really looks like through the layers of makeup. She has long fluffed-out reddish-brown hair and is wearing a denim jacket over an abbreviated cream-coloured buttoned-up sweater that exposes her midriff and fits snugly around her small breasts. Her tight jeans accentuate her slimness, and though Tom can appreciate her figure, he wonders how she can find any comfort in clothes that leave so little room for movement.

"Nice to meet you," he says dutifully. And when he looks into her eyes, what he sees there — dreamy, vacant detachment — reinforces both his sorrow and his desire to be elsewhere.

"Hi," she says brightly.

Tom takes his hand back.

"Want a coffee, Tom?"

"I've had coffee, thanks."

"Well, then let's get this show on the road."

They leave the coffee shop. His father leads the way, one arm gathering Crystal in and holding her close to his side. She giggles as she trips along on three-inch heels.

"How's Mom doing?"

"Oh, you know. I told her we was coming to see her but nothing much sinks in. She has her good days and her bad days, just like the rest of us."

Tom shrugs. "I didn't know that. You never said anything before."

"Well, Tom, it wasn't mine to tell. She could've called you up any time she wanted. I left it up to her. Don't be so touchy with your old man."

"Sorry. But it would have been nice to know. That's all."

His father doesn't elaborate.

Tom follows them through several doors, up a flight of stairs and into a parking garage, where Crystal opens her purse and extracts a set of keys. She struts quickly ahead of them. Charles Brackett takes a step backward and nudges his son in the ribs.

"Jesus, Tom, ain't she something? I tell you, I can't believe my fucking luck." He grins lewdly and pokes Tom playfully in the chest, but all Tom can see is the gap in the older man's mouth where there used to be a tooth. "Yes, boy. I'll tell you something. A bit of pussy sets a man's soul at peace with itself. You remember that for later when you're horny as hell and you got nowhere to put it but your own fist."

Tom just stares at him, unsure what to say. His heart thunders.

"Shit, Charlie! What are you two waiting for back there? We don't got all day. You said that yourself. Right? *Crystal,* you said, *we don't got all fucking day,* when I was putting on my face. Am I right?"

"Right you are, my dear," Charles calls. To his son he says, "Jesus. Women. Ain't they just that fuckin' hard to take?"

Tom follows his father toward the car that Crystal has unlocked.

"C'mon, Dad," he pleads in a whisper. "What is all this? What's she doing here? Why can't you tell me where we're going? You're making me feel like an idiot."

Charles shakes his head.

"Listen, boyo." He steps up close and points a finger at Tom's nose. "Don't you go throwing a bunch of accusations around like some dumbass. I made the best goddamn job out of this mess that I knew how to make, and it wasn't fucking easy." He stares straight into Tom's eyes, challenging. Tom catches a whiff of stale booze. "None of it was easy. You think leaving you with that old hag down there in the middle of nowhere was easy?"

"I'm not —" But Tom sees there will be no reasoning this morning. He raises his hands to indicate his willingness to let the matter drop. "Okay. Let's go. Let's just go and see Mom."

"Yeah." His father turns away. "Let's just go."

CRYSTAL DRIVES. Tom tries to listen in on their conversation, but the choking and rattling of the car's engine drowns them out. As soon as she started it up he knew what the problem was. The gasket is ready to blow. Any day now.

Other than his father's command to "Buckle up, buster," no words have been directed toward the back seat. When they both light cigarettes, Tom feels a craving to light one himself, but doesn't bother since the car is soon filled with smoke. The floor of the car is littered with ash, butts, crushed coffee cups, candy-bar wrappers, a couple of beer cans. Uneasiness trembles awake in his gut now that the reunion with his mother is imminent. Apprehension tugs at him viscerally. What can he say to her? There are simply too many questions to ask. Crystal takes them across the bridge, tossing the coins into the toll basket while the car is still in motion. Now and then her eyes meet his in the rear-view mirror, and he looks away. He can't fathom this relationship. She's half his father's age, and his father looks ten years older than he actually is. Does she think he's rich? Influential? She couldn't possibly be that dumb. What has his father told her about himself? And about the rest of them, about his wife and son and daughter?

He sinks into the lumpy upholstery as the thought hits him that this stranger probably knows more about his own family than he does.

They drive past strip malls and warehouses and a lumber-yard. Row after row of squat houses, identical to one another except for the colour of vinyl siding: sky-blue, muddy brown, mustard- or lemon-yellow. Gas stations, convenience stores. Then they take a left turn off the main road. She's a good driver, Tom concedes — cautious, watchful; she doesn't race the lights.

After a series of turns she pulls into the parking lot behind a plain, three-storey red-brick apartment building. A kind of weary drabness prevails. A single spruce tree and some sun-dazed spirea bushes adorn the grounds, which accommodate two other similarly nondescript buildings. It comes as no surprise to Tom that the reunion with his mother would occur in a setting such as this. His family has always lived amidst drabness and squalor. He remembers the old house, with its loose floorboards and peeling wallpaper. His father did some repairs, but never enough. There was an earlier place too, a draughty apartment, just as bad. Why do they always put up with cracked and chipped linoleum, leaky windows, flaking paint, dripping faucets, doors that hang crooked in their jambs, frayed carpet, dampness, cold?

They climb out of the car, Crystal too, as if she's become part of the family. Which, for all Tom knows, she has.

"How long has she lived here?" Tom asks.

"Since she got out," his father says. "Couple years."

"Out," Tom echoes. "Out of where?"

"Loony bin," his father answers. "What did you think? She was taking a vacation in Mexico or something?"

"Sorry. I didn't know."

"Well, now you do."

"Don't you mean *nuthouse,* Charlie?" Crystal asks. Leaning toward Tom, she says, "I think he means nuthouse."

"Oh yeah," his father says. "'S'cuse my freaking French. I mean nuthouse."

"Where did Beverly live while Mom was…gone away?"

His father looks him carefully up and down. "With me. Where the hell else would she live?"

Tom absorbs this, feeling a tightening in his gut. He doesn't answer.

The building has no security features. The door isn't even locked. Tom's father leads them inside, past a panel of mail slots and buzzers, through the inner door and up the stairs. Tom's energy is drained by the soggy heat that descends upon them. The steamy overripe air is still but for the bawling of a child roaring its rage or pain.

Crystal wraps her thin arms around herself. "This place always gives me the willies."

"Shut your trap," Charles snaps.

They stop beside a wooden door with "10" smeared on it in black paint, in small numerals that look like the work of a careless child. All the other doors along the hall have brass numbers tacked neatly in place, in the exact centre, at eye level.

His father knocks. "Becky, you in there? It's Charlie. I got company."

The child's squall has quieted to a whimper. No sounds come from within his mother's apartment. The flutter in Tom's stomach intensifies until he's afraid he might vomit. He pulls in a breath and holds it, hoping no one will notice the sweat on his forehead. His father listens at the door, his head tilted downward. Crystal stands behind him, arms folded, glassy eyed. Tom imagines them frozen forever in these expectant poses.

Then a clatter rings out from behind the door. Charles, appearing to take it as a signal, winks at Tom and twists the doorknob.

They step inside. It's a small, boxy apartment, walls semi-gloss eggshell. Cigarette smoke hangs in the air. In the kitchen, a dead-end alcove to the left of the entryway, the sink is flowing over with soiled dishes. The dusty hardwood floor is strewn with laundry that might or might not be clean: a child's white socks, a green t-shirt, a yellow towel. A few plastic toys lie within sight. The cluttered grubbiness of the place is depressingly familiar. After waiting for this moment for seven years, no sooner is he inside than he can't wait to leave.

"Becky?" his father calls and then ventures further down the hall. "C'mon out now and meet the company."

"She's hiding again," Crystal explains as his father disappears around a corner.

"Hiding?"

"She'll go into a closet or get behind something." She looks at him for just a moment. "It's really too bad. She was okay for a while. But now she's just plain nuts."

"C'mon Becky. Get some clothes on and come meet the company. Crystal's here. You like her. You like her, don't you?"

"Does Beverly really live here too?" Tom whispers, as if the idea were inconceivable.

"Oh yeah. She's around here somewhere. She's okay. Kind of quiet though — you know — for a little kid."

Charles pulls Tom's mother by the arm into the living room. She is an emaciated gnome-like woman with straggly shoulder-length hair and unnervingly shiny and puckered skin. In his memories she looks nothing like this, and he imagines for a fleeting moment — because he knows it's ridiculous — that it's an elaborate hoax and that they've hired this woman to stand in for his real mother. With her blouse hurriedly and unevenly buttoned, and her glasses hanging at a precarious angle, she has about her the desperate, feral wariness of a freshly apprehended criminal. She says nothing, even at his father's urging, and every few seconds tries to yank her arm free of his grip. Even when Tom explains who he is and why he's come, she refuses to meet his eye, jerking her head away indignantly, as if under the impression that they have brought her out and put her on display for no other reason than to make fun of her.

The little girl creeps down the hall and into the room on her own while Tom is trying to talk to his mother. He gradually becomes aware of her eyes on him, silently staring. When he looks at her she is sucking on her fingers, one after the other, proceeding from thumb to pinkie, and back again.

Her eyes show him neither fear nor curiosity, nor anything in between. She is wearing a dirty, threadbare short-sleeved cotton dress. There are shadows of bruising along both arms. Her eerily translucent skin appears vibrant next to her dark lustreless hair, which hangs in a limp, stringy mess down her back. With her eyes still on him she removes her thumb from her mouth, licks the palm of her hand, and holds it out, smiling now, as if proud to show him what she's done.

And then something very close to fear grips him because this is his family. He can't escape them. Even if he got on a bus this afternoon and didn't get off for a week, or a month, or a year. Each moment he would be reminded, simply by the act of running, of what he was running from.

THREE

TOM IS IN LOVE. It happens at a time when he's not looking to fall in love, when thoughts of getting married and raising a family are farthest from his mind.

Four years after the reunion with his mother and sister he moves into the city. He has no difficulty finding work because cars are not meant to last and good mechanics are always in demand. He asks a fair wage and, much to his surprise, receives it. Suddenly he can afford a small apartment of his own instead of camping out on a friend's sofa. Within a month of leaving his grandmother's house, he is settled.

His apartment on North Street is within sight of the Angus L. Macdonald Bridge. The building is a hundred years old, at one time a stately private residence, now just another Victorian house suffering the indignity of clumsy, ramshackle additions and dirty vinyl siding. His third-floor apartment is so draughty in winter it's like living in a tent on the Commons. The pipes sing; the windows rattle whenever the wind blows. Tom doesn't care. It was his decision to come here, so he'll take the bad with the good and not complain. He enjoys his new routine, the discoveries that come with living someplace different, the daily tide of meaningless events that carries him along with it.

He is not a deep thinker and he knows it, but it has occurred to him that he comes from a family that contributes nothing to the society in which they live. Any time of the day — it might be while taking the bus across town in the morning or picking up groceries after work or just walking the streets for something to do — he can observe men in clean coats and pressed pants, women leading neat and well-behaved children to school or daycare, countless people who toil for wages and pay taxes and keep their homes in respectable condition, and he can't help seeing in his mind his grandmother sitting at the kitchen table in that old house, smoking cigarettes and leafing through magazines, waiting to die, his mother shrunken and distrustful in front of the blaring television in the patients' lounge at the hospital. The last time he spoke to his father was when the older man showed up at Clyde's Esso at noontime on a rainy day, staggering drunk and demanding money. Tom withdrew twenty dollars from the automatic teller and put him in a taxi. Since moving to town he has twice visited Beverly at the foster home where she's been placed. Sulky and morose, she barely spoke to him the first time and the second time refused to come out of her room. Now he phones the foster family once a week to check on how she's doing and wonders if he will ever see her again; wonders to his shame if he even wants to see her again.

If there is anything missing from his life it is friendship, or, more precisely, intimacy and companionship. His friends from school are gone: Alfie and Shirley had a baby and moved to Toronto, Susan married someone Tom's never met, and Barry found a job with the oil rigs in Alberta. Working at a gas station, opportunities to meet women are rare. Uncomplaining, he puts in longer hours than the older mechanics, as well as whatever overtime is asked of him. He sometimes meets people from work to go to a movie or to a bar, but large gatherings make him uncomfortable and finding things to talk about to fill awkward silences is not a talent he possesses. His reluctance to commit himself in a relationship, romantic or otherwise, is conspicuous, even to himself, and makes no sense because it is a large city with a vast population of unattached women and young men who share his interest in hockey and beer and shooting pool. But his small-town diffidence marks him like a physical deformity and stands, in all its ungainly priggishness, between him and emotional familiarity.

On a windy Saturday near the end of October he visits his mother in the Nova Scotia Hospital, where she has resided on and off for much of the time since Tom was sent away, and where, he suspects, she will see the last of her days. The grey and angular structure is imposing and intimidating.

Each time he climbs the concrete steps to the main entrance it is with the restless foreboding that he will be mistaken for an inmate and never again see the outside world. He signs the book and obtains his visitor's pass from the silent guard at the front desk, then proceeds up one flight and down an echoing corridor to the east wing, the minimum security ward where the patients pose no threat to themselves or to anyone else. This is the home of the forlorn and the mute, the harmless lunatic, the untreatable schizoid, the skittish anorexic, the teenage mumbler riding an endless cycle of mood swings. From a few feet away some of them could just about pass for normal; they could be merchants, fire-fighters, ballerinas, students on furlough, housewives taking a break from it all. But when you take a closer look there is always something off-kilter: a trickle of saliva at the corner of the lips, a tremor in the extremities, one eye cocked permanently to some unseen horizon. His mother shares a bare room with three other women close to her in age — mid to late forties; shares with them as well that amorphous, all-encompassing ailment known as chronic depression.

He takes his place beside her on the patched corduroy sofa in front of the television in the day room. The television is old and the reception is poor. But his mother and the others don't move their eyes from the screen. It is a game show filled with whoops and laughter, spinning wheels and glittering lights. Fed up with the flash and glitz, Tom shifts his gaze to the window, to the overcast sky looming above the barricade

of evergreens, and is surprised by a sharp longing for brief
winter days, for the benign disorder of snow, for the tangible
consolation of a normal family. The wind comes up and the
trees sway in the breeze. Nearby, a foursome of male patients
plays a card game. The crackle of their laughter interrupts his
musings, distracting him from his emotions. Tom's mother
giggles during a newscast, for no reason that he can see. She
is haggard, dishevelled; a real mess, his father would have
bluntly observed. They have shorn her hair close to the scalp
and her skin has assumed the bloated, waxy sheen of the
habitually medicated. She does not acknowledge her son.
It is as if she labours under the belief that this youthful,
muscular body seated next to hers has emerged unbidden
out of a dream. She seems to drift about in some alternative realm, a place close to the soul where the only contact
that counts is with oneself. He has tried to reach out to her.
In good weather he's taken her on long walks. The hospital
grounds are extensive and range from the wire fence enclos-
ing a military compound to the stone wall that marks the
perimeter of a residential area. Between these markers lie
several acres of field and forest that his mother will traverse,
but without showing much curiosity in, or even awareness
of, the well-worn path they follow. Early on he used to talk
to her almost incessantly, about his life and the events of
the day. On rare occasions she spoke to him, and he would
lean in to listen to her words, as if still hopeful that after all
these years a glimpse into her state of mind was imminent.

"Fix the clock," she would command, gesturing toward a crow perched on the limb of a tall pine. "Fix the clock!" Or perhaps she'd confide, with a cunning nod, "They came in the middle of the night with peanuts, but I wouldn't eat any." His frustration with her disjointed utterances has so often left him trembling that most days now he keeps quiet, enduring her silence and her outbursts with simple resignation.

After an hour of television he retrieves his wallet from an inner pocket of his jacket. Leaving the jacket draped over his place on the sofa so his mother will know he's coming back — if she even notices he's gone — he heads out the door and down the long corridor. The cafeteria for visitors and staff is in the basement. Tom descends the stairs hopeful that the girl will once again be there.

She glances up from an outdated copy of *Chatelaine,* smiles when she sees him, and places the magazine to one side. As he draws near to her his heart lurches to a stop, then stutters back into motion like some wounded engine. The cafeteria is a wide, bleak room starkly lit by rows of fluorescent lights that create a harsh glare against cinderblock walls painted shiny orange. Concrete floor, ancient tables, plastic chairs with tubular metal legs. Her name is Kathleen.

"Hi," Tom says. He pulls out the chair across from her.

"How's your mom today?" Kathleen asks. Her eyes are wide and gracious.

"The same," he says. "She's always the same. Nothing ever changes."

This is only the third time they've spoken. He was already conscious of her presence two or three weeks before making himself sit at her table. Others might think she is too thin and pale to be attractive, and fault her for her long brown hair that has no shine to it. But what Tom sees is a young woman with delicate features and clear skin and huge eyes that light up whenever he looks into them; a young woman who might share his warped vision of what passes for normal.

He looks into her eyes and asks, "What about your sister?"

She shrugs and casts him a wistful smile. "Well, at least she didn't try to kill herself again last night."

Tom nods. This is good news because Kathleen's sister Abby has tried to kill herself many times with whatever instrument happens to be at hand. At home she tried it with pills and razor blades. In the psych ward at the Children's Hospital in Halifax she tied a bed sheet around her neck and tried to hang herself from a light fixture. Her first night in the Nova Scotia Hospital she smashed her head against the wall until she bled. Now she's refusing to eat, which, he decides, is not exactly like trying to kill yourself. Maybe she's not hungry.

"I mean, you still can't talk to her or anything. But at least she's out of the cage ... you know, that room with the grill in the door. It's not so bad when she's with us and sitting up in bed. I turned the TV on and we watched part of a movie. They started her on lithium, I think. Something like that."

"Do they think she might get out of here someday?"

"They're not saying. My dad's really upset. First Mom, now this."

Sometime within the past year Kathleen's mother killed herself. Tom nods. He has not asked for the details and she has not offered.

"Do you want a coffee or anything?"

Tom gets them both coffee and resumes his seat. He feels weightless in this girl's presence. Even with his mother confined upstairs, his father on the street panhandling for booze money, and his sister groping through a darkness all her own, he cannot resist the contentment that suffuses him like sunlit warmth whenever Kathleen's eyes find his.

"It's weird, because she was always the happy one when we were kids. She never seemed to get depressed and she was always laughing at something. She liked making up stories, and she read lots of books. She was always going places in her head and imagining stuff. Not in a bad way, like she was crazy or anything. But more like how you think of someone writing a book, putting in little things so that it all seems real. She could do that."

"I do that sometimes," Tom admits, realizing for the first time that his inclination to daydream might result from an impulse more noble than simply idleness and boredom. "Not make things up, but sort of drift away. If I'm working on a car and it's something I do all the time, like changing oil, I'll just pretend I'm somewhere else."

"Where do you go when you do that?" Kathleen asks. "Like, where would you want to be, if you had a choice?"

With you, he feels like saying.

"Well, I've never been anywhere, and I don't read about places, so I guess...." His answer strikes him as juvenile and unimaginative. "I guess I keep going home, back to when I was little, before my mother got sick. We had a nice enough place. My dad had a decent job. We lived in a small town and I had a lot of friends. We'd go skating in the winter and play ball in the summer."

"That's a good place to be," Kathleen says. "Home, I mean."

"But now it's almost like it never happened. Or like it happened to someone else and I just heard about it or saw it on TV. I can't believe I was ever part of a family that lived in the same house together."

"You have to believe in something," Kathleen says, and slumps back in her chair. "My Dad says that. You have to believe that things will get better or else you might as well just give up."

They sit in silence for a moment. A group of hospital staff on break enters the cafeteria and the chatter of conversation washes over them.

"None of us knew there was anything wrong with Mom," Kathleen says suddenly, her eyes focused on her fingers wrapped around the cafeteria mug. "We were all so worried about Abby. She was being weird — scary weird. You know? Everything about her was dark. She wore black all the time, and dyed her hair black and wore black nail polish. All she ever said was *fuck this* or *fuck that,* or give you this look like you were nuts when you tried to talk to her about anything. But Mom didn't change. She was still, like, you know, Mom. The day she died she made apple pies, three of them, one for each of us I guess. And there was a pot of soup on the stove, beef and barley. She made all this stuff in the morning and cleaned up the mess and then went into the garage and got in the car and ran the engine until she was dead. Abby found her. We all thought there had to be a note, but there wasn't any. She never said anything about being tired or sad. It was like...." In desperation she searches the room and then lowers her eyes. When she raises her head she asks, "How can you be ready for something like that?"

"Hey, it's okay," Tom says helplessly. He pulls a tissue from his pocket, but it's soiled and crumpled, so he puts it away again.

Kathleen wipes some tears with her hand. "I'm sorry," she says. "I shouldn't be talking about this."

"No. I don't mind." Then he says, "It's always better if you don't keep it all inside."

She blows her nose using a serviette. Tom wants to respond in a way that will inspire her confidence and trust, but doesn't know how. He wonders if this is where their ease with each other, built and strengthened over these last weeks, will begin to erode. All of his dealings with women have foundered and perished on awkwardness, unable to survive his inability to put thoughts into words. Fearful of being boring, he sticks with the cloddish silence of the socially inept. In high school this diffidence killed his relationship with Mary Ann Beddoes, whose precocious hormones and accommodating nature made it possible for him to lose his virginity at sixteen one winter afternoon on the couch in her basement. Later, after she lost interest in his stubborn silences and moved over to a faster crowd, he started playing psychological games with himself, trying to master the thickening of his tongue in the presence of women his own age. But still the words refused to come, or else emerged foolish and stumbling: like tender progeny with no chance of survival.

"I've scared you," Kathleen says resignedly, her eyes still wet. "Now you think I'm weird or some loser from a family of wackos."

Tom shakes his head. He turns toward the window. In the parking lot a rust-dotted Oldsmobile pulls into a space. A balding man in a grey windbreaker climbs from the car, and with his arms clenched tightly across his chest struggles against the wind. He disappears around the corner.

"My family is every bit as crazy as yours," Tom says finally. "Maybe crazier." He shrugs and turns to look into Kathleen's eyes. "I can't do anything about it. I just want to get on with my life."

She nods, apparently grateful for his honesty. Has he said the right thing? Tom, his heart thundering, reaches across the table. Kathleen accepts his hand. He squeezes her fingers, sensing the frailty of her being in each tiny bone.

IAN COLFORD

UPSTAIRS A FEW MINUTES later, having met Kathleen's father (the man in the windbreaker) and with Kathleen's phone number written on a scrap of paper in his wallet, Tom collects his jacket from the sofa in front of the television. His mother has moved, or been moved, to a straight-backed chair and is staring out of one of the floor-to-ceiling windows that permits a view of the grounds and, beyond these, the harbour.

He touches her shoulder. His hand is still trembling. Outside, leaves dance and swirl on the wet grass.

"Hey, Mom?"

She doesn't move.

"I'm going now. I'll see you in a couple of weeks."

She makes no response. Tom leans over to look into her eyes. It's like looking through a doorway into an empty room.

FOUR

THE REALITY OF GROWING OLDER catches Tom Brackett by surprise. One morning he pauses to study his face in the mirror and realizes with a start that he's married, mortgaged, a father, though he still feels seventeen. It's inconceivable, but there it is.

After he and Kathleen marry, her father helps them with the down payment on a small house in a tidy suburb twenty minutes or so outside the city. He is grateful, but wishes he had been able to manage the purchase unaided. Still, their first home, and on the day they move in with their meagre assortment of mismatched belongings, they make love on the futon before taking anything out of the boxes. Kathleen runs naked to the bathroom and Tom follows, and they make love again in the shower. She laughs with her mouth wide open. Her playful irreverence delights him; her crooked smile inspires his protectiveness and feeds his lust. He sets up his bodybuilding equipment in the basement and Kathleen installs a loom, an ancient clattering relic passed down through many hands to the present day. As he watches her pass the weft thread, wound around the shuttle, back and forth and back and forth, watches the brightly patterned cloth emerge like magic from a tangle of twine, watches as she stops to make minute and arcane adjustments, he wonders how anyone can have such patience. He observes her adoringly. She is his Kathleen. Thin, but lithe, like a cat; timid among strangers but mischievous in bed. He pumps his weights.

Tom continues to work at the South Street Esso, where he is now a senior mechanic. He is the one to whom the rookies come for advice, the one whose talent and proficiency the regular customers rely upon. It occurs to him one day that all this expertise and dedication must be valuable, so he asks his boss, station owner Clyde Harrow, for a raise. He doesn't have to ask twice. He knows he is fortunate to enjoy what he does and to work for someone he can respect. After all these years he can still hear his father complaining about the shitheads at the lumberyard, telling him stories about how they tried to break up the union with hammers and baseball bats. There's so much he doesn't have to put up with.

For both of them life becomes a routine of working and sleeping. Kathleen toys with the idea of university, but abandons the notion forever when she discovers the expenses involved. Instead she enrols in a series of computer courses at the community college and takes a part-time job as a cash clerk at Sobeys, the lowest of the low, hating every minute. He can see the tension in her brow and hear it in her voice when he picks her up after work. One day she is crying, but won't answer him when he asks what's wrong. She works on her loom the way he lifts weights, testing her stamina, seeing how long she can stay with it. He notices that she doesn't seem to be spending enough time on her assignments and suspects that she's not studying for tests, but reserves comment. One day she stops going to her classes, sells her textbooks, and begins full-time at Sobeys. The decision is never addressed, never discussed.

When they discover she is pregnant, Tom conceals twinges of dread beneath outrageous bursts of generosity and feverish displays of optimism. He buys gifts for Kathleen, for his father-in-law, for Abby, who has moved back home with her dad. He phones Beverly at the halfway house, where she's working off her community service on a shoplifting charge, to tell her she's going to be an aunt. He even tells his mother and allows himself to believe that her lips curl upward at the corners ever so slightly at the news. He tells the boys at work, friends, people in the neighbourhood he hardly knows. He can't stop smiling. But the truth is that fatherhood is something he never expected for himself. He can't see himself in that role, doesn't know how to prepare for it, and wonders if he'll ever be ready. Still, his pleasure is impossible to contain; he catches himself grinning at odd moments for no reason. He becomes the caricature of the expectant father, solicitous to a fault, until Kathleen informs him she's not due for another eight months and thank you but she's perfectly able to open the car door for herself.

He has not seen his father for five years. Kathleen has never met him or even seen a photograph of him. So when Tillie Ferguson from down home phones to tell him of his grandmother's sudden death from a heart attack, he uses the news as an excuse to look for his father, but isn't able to determine if he's still in the city. He visits the street corner where his father used to solicit spare change, but there is no sign of him. He makes a few calls: the shelters, the soup kitchens, social services. Nothing. The people he speaks to have either never heard of him or only remember him vaguely, and can't say when they last saw him. It occurs to him to look for Crystal instead, but then he realizes that he never learned her last name. And he suspects that relationship didn't last very long anyway. Tom can't quite shake the feeling that he's to blame. He had every right to move forward with his life, but he's also the only member of his family with any trace of responsibility. He should have kept an eye on things.

Tillie puts him in touch with Reverend Michaels at the Presbyterian Church so he can make arrangements for the funeral. It's up to him to see his grandmother safely into her final resting place and to sort out her belongings. He tells Kathleen that it will only take a couple of days to drive out there and settle up his grandmother's affairs, but she wants to go too. It's a part of him that she's heard about but never seen. Ancient history, he says, gruffly dismissing her curiosity. "But it's your history," she replies, obviously annoyed, "and like it or not, that includes me now." He just looks at her. He's not about to get into a fight over this.

The drive along the south shore to Liverpool is longer than he remembers, though once they arrive, it turns out to be not very long at all, and he wonders why he always felt too busy to make the trip when his grandmother was alive.

Tom has been paying his grandmother's bills and seeing to her needs, a responsibility that fell to him by default when his father pulled his vanishing act. There was no warning. One day he made his weekly call to find that her number was no longer in service, and he realized his father had abandoned her too. He increased his calls to twice a week, but as neither of them had much to say the calls were brief and strained. He's kept in touch with a few people in the area, making sure someone was stopping in from time to time. Tillie Ferguson called him every other week or so. Mary Ellen Barker, a retiree whose house was a mile or so up the road, went over regularly to make sure the older woman had enough in the cupboard to keep her alive. Before stopping by his grandmother's place, he pulls in at Mary Ellen's, just to get a feel for what's been going on. She greets him with a whoop and a hug, and, when he introduces Kathleen, hugs her too.

"Things haven't changed much around here, have they?" Tom comments as Mary Ellen ushers them into her modest two-storey home. A faintly sweet aroma hovers in the air along with the background drone of a radio. Tom struggles to remember the name of Mary Ellen's husband, but before he embarrasses them all by asking after him, the thought comes that he might be dead.

"Some things change and some things stay the same," Mary Ellen says cheerfully. "I can see there's been a change or two in your life."

"Yeah, a couple of years now," Tom says.

Mary Ellen turns to Kathleen. "I hope you know, dear, that you've married a real hell raiser."

Kathleen laughs. "Oh, really?" They make eye contact and Tom shrugs and looks away.

"Yes, always breaking things and getting into trouble. That's our Tom."

"Well, not really," Tom says, flustered. "There was —"

"A right handful for old Thelma, I can tell you. But she did her best. There's not much that a woman of seventy can do with a youngster. Just feeding one can be enough to do you in these days."

"Oh, I hope not," Kathleen says, and then pats her still flat tummy.

"Oh, my. Really?" Mary Ellen asks, wide-eyed. "You can't tell yet, that's for sure."

"Another few months," Tom says, his enthusiasm for this visit on the wane.

"Well now, come on in and sit yourself down."

In the parlour they settle in to the ritual of tea and home-baked cookies. Kathleen eats five ginger snaps and half a dozen shortbreads. Mary Ellen recites the news of the town, who's married and who's dead, who's out of business and who's moved away. She doesn't mention her husband — Robert, Tom remembers. Robert was the postmaster. And, yes, he is dead, a few years now. It was sudden: a heart attack. His grandmother told him.

The house is filled with knick-knacks, five-and-dime figurines, family photos in plastic frames, tole-painted tables and lampshades: things that collect dust but never break or get lost or wear out. Their own house is sterile by comparison, with its bare walls and empty shelves. Tom excuses himself to use the bathroom and once upstairs pauses beside a window that overlooks the backyard. The day is early April grey with a soft drizzle descending. Huge and unruly, the yard reminds him of the acre or two of soggy pasture behind his grandmother's place, that was either flooded or growing wild with thistles or tall stringy grass, depending on the season, but where, he'd been told, cows used to graze. At the edge of the lot is a red barn collapsing in on itself, all that remains of Mary Ellen's country store and antique shop. He and Alfie would go in to buy candy after the school bus let them off, and he remembers with stunning clarity pocketing a chocolate bar right out from under Mary Ellen's nose, thinking he'd done so well to get away with it. Only now, fifteen years later, does he realize that Mary Ellen probably saw what he did and said nothing, to save his grandmother, and no doubt herself, the shame of a confrontation.

When he returns to the parlour the expression on Kathleen's face ties a knot in his gut.

"Tom, your father's in town."

"What?" He looks at Mary Ellen, who raises one hand as if shielding herself.

"I'm only saying what I've been told. I never saw him myself, but Tillie says she was going by Thelma's place and there he was coming out of the house carrying something, looked like a suitcase, she said. But it was getting dark so she couldn't tell for sure."

"When was this?" Tom asks, and then, "How does she know it was him?"

"Yesterday. There's no mistaking Charlie. He's got that walk."

Tom nods.

"Is he still around? Do you know if he's staying out there?"

"I don't know anything for sure. But if he's not at the house I'd guess he's in one of those motels down the road." Mary Ellen looks at Tom sympathetically and says, "I gather you don't see much of your dad these days?"

Tom resumes his place on the sofa next to Kathleen and takes a cookie off the tray. He stares at it but doesn't eat it.

"I tried, but it wasn't easy." He doesn't want to admit that his father's been living like a bum, that when he stopped showing up at the station looking for money, Tom was relieved. "It was only when Gran died that I started thinking how long it's been." Tom shakes his head and bites the thin end off the cookie. "Years."

"How's Rebecca?"

"The same."

"And Beverly?"

Tom looks up and shrugs. "She was picked up for shoplifting a while ago. She dropped out of school. We wanted her to come and live with us but she...." He laughs and shakes his head. "God, my family's such a mess."

Kathleen takes his hand into hers.

"It's not your fault, Tommy." Mary Ellen's voice makes it sound like the truth. "Your mother's a sad case and can't be helped. But the others, well, it's not up to you or me to tell someone else how to live their life. You can't get yourself into a stew just because your father can't hold a job or your sister looks at things the wrong way. Think of yourself and your lovely wife and that baby that's coming."

Tom and Kathleen squeeze each other's hands, but after this the conversation falters and sputters like an old Chevy with a clogged fuel line. Tom feels exposed and vulnerable, the heat of an inexplicable resentment warming his neck as if he's been coerced into revealing more than he intended. Everyone is sated with tea and cookies and the long afternoon. Tom uses the phone in the kitchen to check in with Reverend Michaels about the funeral. The priest assures him that everything is in hand, and without Tom asking for details informs him that his grandmother did not suffer, that she died instantly of a sudden paralysis of the heart muscles, and that the fact of her death was widely known very soon after it happened because the boy from the Save-Easy was out delivering groceries that day. Visitation is tomorrow at Patterson's Funeral Home. Today is Saturday; the funeral is set for Monday morning, ten o'clock.

He and Kathleen still have to find somewhere to stay, but he's not about to bring this up because Mary Ellen would make the obvious offer and probably insist, and then they'd be stuck.

His father's unexpected presence here fills him with the same kind of dread that would afflict him on the walk to school when he hadn't done his homework or had neglected to study for a test he had to write. On those mornings anxiety seeped from his pores and his heart hammered so loudly he was sure everyone could hear it. As he returns to the parlour and signals to Kathleen that it's time to leave, the familiar feeling comes over him of having been derelict in some duty. He feels like he's bungled the job and is now face to face with his comeuppance. He doesn't understand why he's reacting this way because he wanted his father to be here — it is a family occasion, this sending off — and even hunted for him with the intention of persuading him to come. But it's been taken out of his hands and he can't begin to guess what kind of bombshell his father will drop on him this time.

Worn out from the drive and the visit, they agree that going by the house can wait until tomorrow. Ten minutes further along the highway is a roadside motel that looks less run-down than the others but is called, ominously, the EconoLodge. It isn't until they get to their room that Tom feels the full weight of exhaustion bearing down on him. He avoids Kathleen's eyes, and when he fails to respond to a succession of wry comments — about Mary Ellen, about the town, about the weather — she falls silent too. While Kathleen takes a shower he lies on the bed and with his arm covering his eyes envisions the boy he used to be. There he is, outfitted in shabby rummage-sale clothes, always either too big or too small, wandering down the road or through the woods looking for something to relieve the boredom of those endless summer afternoons. Alone, almost always alone, and not just because his friends live too far away but because they've been warned about the old woman who lives in the middle of the woods, and anyway his grandmother doesn't want "strangers" in her house. And — let's face it — he doesn't invite them because he's ashamed for them to see where he lives. So, idle and alone, he spends entire afternoons tossing rocks at birds and squirrels, teasing dogs tethered to stakes in junk-littered yards, climbing trees to see how high he can get, exploring the collapsed remnants of an abandoned farmhouse. At the highway overpass he leans on the railing and counts the cars. Down at the beach he kills time looking for shells, combing through the garbage washed up on shore and skimming stones. Later he lingers in front of houses where he's learned that if he lets himself be seen the people might — if they don't chase him away — give him something to eat. It's not that his grandmother starves him. But sometimes, sitting down for a meal, he catches a whiff of mildew or rot, and it's enough to make the food she puts in front of him seem as old and decrepit as everything else. When he finally comes home, well after dark, she's right where he left her, at the kitchen table. She gazes at him from behind a veil of smoke, perhaps offering a vacant smile, most times looking right through him.

IN THE MORNING, battling a smouldering reluctance, Tom drives with Kathleen to the house. It is a dreary day, wet with persistent drizzle. This afternoon they have to visit the funeral home and select a casket for the visitation. He's never been through anything like this before. Kathleen has, and so he looks to her for answers, deferring to her greater experience in these matters that leave him confounded and sweaty with indecision.

When they pull up in front of his grandmother's house Tom, aware of Kathleen beside him, sees how derelict the simple two-storey building has become. It looks as if nobody has lived there for years. In desperate need of paint and nails to hold them in place, innumerable shingles have slipped away, leaving blackened gaps in the siding. Of the four front windows, two have been covered with plywood panels that are grey with age.

They get out of the car and approach the front veranda, which sags beneath Tom's weight when he ascends the steps.

"Tom, please be careful!" Kathleen folds her arms and backs off a few paces.

"It's okay," he says calmly. The unpainted planks under his feet are soft with rot. He tries the door. It's not locked.

"Coming in?"

Inside they are assailed by a pervasive but stubbornly elusive odour that fills their nostrils with the sogginess of trapped air and the overly sweet mustiness of fermentation. Kathleen tips her nose upward. Tom sniffs and peers up the narrow flight of stairs — so much narrower than it appears in his memories — as if the answer to the mystery is waiting on the second floor, though it could be anywhere: the parlour ahead of them to the right, the dining room, or the kitchen at the end of the hall.

Tom shakes his head. "This feels so weird," he says. He meets Kathleen's eye and smiles awkwardly. Having her with him is what he's referring to, the mingling of past and present to create something that is neither.

As they proceed from room to room, Tom senses keenly the absence of objects he fully expected to find, antiques he'd been told arrived with ancestral immigrants more than a hundred years ago: the roll-top desk, a pair of ornate brass candlesticks, a wrought-iron floor lamp, a couple of Victorian clocks, a cedar chest, a silver tea set, the age-darkened painting of ships in harbour — these are gone. The walls are completely bare. The built-in corner cabinet in the dining room is empty of china, the dining-room table itself is missing, though the eight chairs remain, lined up against the wall.

Upstairs it is the same. His grandmother's bedroom has been cleared out. The other bedroom, which used to be Tom's, contains a few cardboard boxes filled with photograph albums, paperback books, bedding, towels.

"I don't get it," he says. He follows Kathleen down the stairs. "It's like she was moving out or something."

"Maybe she knew she was dying and wanted to be ready so she started packing things up."

Tom just looks at her.

"I don't know," Kathleen says, turning momentarily defensive. "I've heard that there are people who can tell, you know, when the end is coming. If they're really sick. They get sensitive or something."

Tom shrugs.

"I don't think she *was* sick. And besides, that doesn't explain where all this stuff went."

"Maybe she gave it to people, the ones who helped her."

Tom considers this for a moment before shaking his head.

"Somebody would have told me. And anyway, if she started giving things away for no reason people would've thought she was crazy. Nobody would've actually taken anything. They would've guessed something was wrong. People watch out for each other here, you know. It's not like in the city."

Kathleen wilts beneath this casual reproof but stays with Tom as he goes back into the parlour. Tom takes a mental inventory of what's left: a matching sofa and armchair, both so old the flowered pattern is a ghost of itself; a square coffee table, chipped at all four corners, some flimsy metal shelves for ornaments. The room is swathed in shadow because one of the windows is covered with plywood, but around the casings Tom can easily follow the tracery of creeping water stains. The kitchen has received a thorough cleaning; by whose hand there is no way to tell, though Tom suspects the women of the community after his grandmother's death. The top of the stove and the oven are spotless. There is nothing in the refrigerator. Curiously, there is little evidence of his grand-mother's occupancy, though she lived here for fifty years.

Then they hear the rumble of another vehicle. Tom goes to the uncovered window at the front of the house. It's turned brighter. The drizzle has stopped and the sun is starting to poke through the grey. Tom watches a burnt-red, rust-pocked pick-up truck veer onto the bare patch of mud beside his Toyota. A burly, bearded man emerges from the driver's side. Then the passenger door opens.

Kathleen is beside him. "Who is it?"

Tom laughs and shakes his head. Perhaps he's been ex-pecting this, or something like this, all along.

"It's my dad," he says, pointing. "Him, the skinny one."

"Who's the other guy?"

"Don't know him."

They watch as the two men enter into a discussion. Tom's father gestures toward the house while the other man seems distracted by Tom's car, which he looks at as if it presents a prob-lem he doesn't quite know how to deal with. Finally, with a curt nod, the burly man returns to the truck, starts it up, and begins backing it toward the house. Pointing and rotating his arm, Charles Brackett directs the way around the Toyota and over the grass. Though it's still early, Tom can see that his father has been drinking. The almost ceremonial caution with which he navigates his way around the stones littering the lawn resem-bles the slow progress of a man wading through deep water.

"What do you think they're doing?"

"I can guess," Tom says and steadies his mind and his body for the inevitable confrontation. He does not ask himself why it must be this way. It simply is.

"Should we go?"

"Soon," he says.

The truck jerks to a stop just as he steps outdoors.

"Hi Dad," he says.

"Thought that was your junk bucket piece of crap," Charles Brackett says as he turns and places one hand on the truck to steady himself. The other man cuts the engine and gets out.

"That car's new. You've never seen it before."

"You don't know shit about what I seen and what I ain't seen."

Tom does not respond to his father's manner or tone. Expelling a breath, he glances toward the sky, where patches of blue have appeared amidst the scattering cover of clouds. Then, reluctantly, he shifts his gaze back to his father. The older man's face beneath his dirty cap is almost fully obscured by shadow, but this does not disguise the bristly grey whiskers and the wrinkles incised so deeply into the skin they could be battle scars.

"You're looking good. Where have you been keeping yourself these days?"

"Keeping myself, am I?" Over his shoulder, Charles addresses his companion, whose thick-lipped mouth broadens into a smile. "Keeping myself, the man says." He chuckles. "Keeping myself."

"It's just a question, Dad."

"Well, looks like I ain't been keeping myself anywheres you can find me."

Tom shrugs. "I guess you're right. When I heard that Gran died I went looking all over town to see if you needed a lift up here. But I can see I didn't need to worry myself."

"Tom, we should go."

Kathleen is behind and then beside him, imploring with liquid eyes. Both her voice and the hand wrapped around his arm are trembling.

"Dad, I want you to meet my wife, Kathleen. Honey, meet my Dad."

"Hello, Mr. Brackett." Kathleen's voice hovers just within the range of audibility. "I'm pleased to meet you."

Charles squints in Kathleen's direction and adjusts his cap. He says nothing.

For a moment everyone stands still, as if awaiting a director's signal to release them back into action. A chill breeze passes over the scene. Tom feels the tension in the air coil tighter and realizes he's clenched his hands into fists. The absurdity of the situation almost causes him to burst out laughing. Tall weeds shuddering on spindly stalks catch his attention, as does the dog — a black-muzzled boxer — which he hadn't noticed before, sitting placidly upright in the cab of the truck. A few seagulls circling overhead cry mournfully. His nostrils catch the scent of boggy turf swollen with rain. Again he is blindsided by the central reality of his life, that he belongs to a family of thieves, addicts, and lunatics.

"C'mon Jimmy. We got work to do." Tom's father speaks in a cracked, resigned voice. He and Jimmy mount the steps.

Tom moves in front of them. "Hey, whoa! What's going on here?"

Tom understands the risk he's taking. Jimmy looks like a thug who will only land a punch to get himself out of harm's way, but his father will go for blood just for the pleasure of seeing it flow.

"Tom!" Kathleen pleads. "Let them do what they want!"

"All I want," Tom says, addressing his father, "is to know where you're taking this stuff. I think I have a right to know that much."

"You think you have a right, do you?" Charles Brackett fumes. "Well, boy, you got no rights, not where my things is concerned. No sir."

"What makes it yours? Where's the will?"

"There ain't no will."

"What do you mean? There's got to be a will. I know there's a will. She showed it to me once, or showed me where she kept it."

"It wasn't there."

"Wasn't where? In the desk?"

Charles Brackett squeezes his eyes shut, apparently searching his memory for an answer. He opens them again, looks down at the ground, turns and steps toward the truck, then seems to think better of it and turns back to face his son. He raises his chin in the air.

"I tore it up."

"You what?"

"Hey, man," Jimmy says. "You didn't tell me this."

Charles shakes his head. "There weren't nothing in it worth reading."

"Jesus, Dad." Tom locks gazes with his father. "Well, what did it say? Who did she leave everything to?"

Charles chews on the corner of his mouth. "I never read it."

"You never read it?"

"Didn't have to. It's all mine. Lock, stock, and barrel."

"This isn't good, man."

"Jesus, Jimmy! Will you just shut the fuck up! We got to move this shit out of here."

Jimmy holds up his hands and backs off until he's standing behind the truck.

"What's your hurry, Dad?"

Charles's sour expression has turned slack-jawed and distant.

"I'm getting the hell out of town, soon as I get my goddamn money. No one's going to fuck with me anymore."

"What about the funeral?"

"Only goddamn funeral I'm sitting still for is my own." He aims a skinny finger at the house and climbs the steps. "I waited my whole life for this, Tom. My whole fucking life. By Jesus, nobody can tell me I don't deserve it, every last scrap of what's in there. She hung on just to spite me." His glance shifts briefly from Tom to Kathleen. He licks his lips self-consciously, but then makes himself go on. "Just because she knew I was out there. If I'd a died first, she would've kicked off the next day. That's the truth. She could have done this years ago." He nods in agreement with himself. "Who would have knowed any different? I ask you. Except the nosy old cows live 'round here. She never did nothing. Never went anywhere. Goddamn waste of time she was, the old bitch. Letting the place go to stink and rot. So I'm taking it all. Jimmy'll sell it. But I get my money first. That's the deal. Ain't that right, Jimmy?"

"Yeah, Mr. Brackett. That's the deal." Jimmy joins them on the rickety veranda, which sags steeply beneath his weight. "We're paying up front."

"How much?" Tom asks.

"Huh?"

"How much are you giving him for all these things? The furniture, the china, the silver. There was a TV too. I bought it no more than a couple of years ago."

"It's a fair price," Jimmy says, on the defensive. "Five thousand. Up front. He wouldn't get that anywheres else."

Tom senses a rip-off but doesn't know what to say because he has no idea what his grandmother's things might be worth.

"Tom," his father pleads. The truculent drunk has apparently slipped offstage and been replaced by a bony old man who would rather bargain than fight. "Boy. I need the money."

Tom is shocked to speechlessness by the gaunt, slovenly old alcoholic who is asking permission of his son to sell the only items of value the family has ever owned.

"You want the TV back?" Jimmy asks, a note of desperation creeping into his voice and boosting its pitch slightly. "How about I give you the TV back and keep the same price? Can't ask for better than that."

"Listen to the man, son," his father says. "We'll get rid of this crap right now and I'll have money in my hand. Today. That right, Jimmy?"

"That's right Mr. Brackett. Cash. No cheques."

Tom watches his father, who looks down and won't meet his eye. Charles shuffles his feet and thrusts his hands into his pockets. Tom doesn't know the whole story, but that's a familiar feeling. Where his father is concerned he's never had a clear picture. What is unfamiliar is that for the first time Tom can remember, his father has admitted a need. It shakes him, that the old man has been reduced to this. His breath catches in his throat.

"That's fine," he says, managing to keep his voice steady. "But I don't want the TV back. It was brand new when I bought it and it's one of those flat widescreen ones that'll hook up to a stereo system. Cost almost a thousand dollars. How about you keep it and give him five hundred dollars more?"

Jimmy shifts his bulk from one foot to the other. Tom stands next to his father. To Jimmy it would look like they are presenting a united front. Tom hardly knows what to think about that.

"Done," Jimmy says, and thrusts his thick hand in Tom's direction. They shake.

Tom helps Jimmy carry the remaining items from the house and pile them in the back of the truck. After all his resistance he's relieved it's not up to him to decide the fate of these things. It doesn't surprise him to see that, now that his father is getting what he came for, he's become downright friendly, taking Kathleen by the arm and leading her around the mouldering property, as proud as any gentleman farmer, talking loudly, laughing, calling her attention to one thing or another. It's strange to see him so animated. When did he last see his father laugh?

When everything has been loaded and the house is empty, Tom and Jimmy pause on the veranda to catch their breath. Kathleen and Charles join them. The sun peeks out from behind the clouds. Tom catches a few seconds of feeble warmth. He'll have to hire a real estate agent to sell what's left: the house, which is worthless, and the property, which might bring in a few thousand. He'll give the money to his dad. When he tells his father this, Charles smiles and briefly nods his acceptance. His eyes shimmer as he looks down and then turns and gazes out toward the road. For the second time today Tom is shaken. Could the old man actually be proud of him?

FIVE

THE CASUAL OBSERVER would envy the serene and stable existence Tom Brackett has fashioned for himself. He and Kathleen live in apparent harmony in a large house on a corner lot in Hammonds Plains with their two children: Hannah, who is eight, and Charlie, five. They have a golden retriever named Sammy. Tom drives to the South Street Esso each morning and more often than not puts in a ten-hour day. Kathleen stays at home. With the mortgage paid off, there's no need for her to take a job in order to supplement their income. Instead, their early sacrifices mean she has been able to raise both children from infancy and that she is present when they arrive for lunch and when they get home after school, a situation that both parents regard as healthier than placing them into the hands of strangers in a daycare facility. In her spare hours she works at her loom and displays the results of her labour at a craft store in town.

After getting the money from the sale of the house, Tom's father fell out of his life, irretrievably, like a stone dropped into deep water. Tom occasionally wonders what he's done with himself, but mourning his father's absence is not something on which he expends a great deal of mental or emotional energy. In fact, he sometimes finds himself inwardly celebrating what appears to be the nearly clean break he has made from his family, shying away from speculation regarding the sort of influence they might have had on his children as figures on the horizon of their young lives, or as a daily presence that would have to be acknowledged or explained. Tom visits his mother in the hospital from time to time, but for now is content to let his children believe that she is dead. Someday he will confess his deception and they will feel cheated and confront him with righteous and reasonable bitterness, but at the moment his opinion is that introducing them to their aggressively medicated and intermittently conscious grandmother would add nothing to their lives.

As for Beverly, the roller-coaster ride continues. A full year in which his sister lived free of booze and drugs seduced him into hoping that she had straightened out once and for all. Encouraged, he kept his distance, didn't intrude or push any harder than she was pushing herself. As tempting as it would have been to do so, it was something she had to accomplish on her own. When she slipped, he kept his hope alive by convincing himself it was a temporary setback. Foolishly, as it turns out. Because lately she appears to have picked up the trail of her former addictions as if they were unfinished business.

His hopes all but dead, he has discovered within himself a capacity for meanness: a terrible wish that she will overdose and let him get on with his life.

There is a lunch diner located in the office building on the street behind the Esso station. Tom slides into a booth and orders a coffee while he waits for his sister. Their meetings always take place, at her request, in some neutral setting, covertly. He'll go home and at some point during the evening will say to Kathleen, "I saw Beverly today." To which Kathleen will respond, "Oh, and how is she?" And Tom will say, "The same," which means nothing because she is never exactly the same from one meeting to the next, though the differences are often subtle and tricky to isolate. But Kathleen knows better than to inquire further or to suggest he bring Beverly home for a visit or a meal.

It is hot outside but pleasantly cool in the restaurant. When his coffee arrives, he taps a cigarette out of the pack and for a moment holds it, unlit, between his fingers before placing it on the table. He's brought an extra pack to give to his sister and, over and above the bank withdrawal he has made specifically for her, he has enough money in his wallet to pay for two lunches. As he spots her climbing with loose-limbed ease from a taxi, he tells himself it's a case of charity. He's generous. He likes to help people. In any situation, he wants to do the right thing. But his baby sister will never be as tractable as those representatives of organizations who phone and then politely hang up when you tell them sorry but you just can't afford to help them out this year. This charity never goes away and won't take no for an answer.

Beverly still wears mostly black, a fashion choice that does her no favours because, in combination with the abnormal paleness of her skin, the creases around her mouth, and the exaggerated lines of mascara circling her eyes, it produces an alarming gauntness that can't entirely be blamed on thirty years of hard living. Her short hair, which used to be as black as shoe polish, is today streaked with grey.

She flops distractedly into the booth and glances at him across the table as she removes her leather jacket, which, Tom notes, he has never seen before.

"Got something to say?"

Tom shrugs. He notes as well the flaking skin ringing her nostrils, the dilated pupils.

"As always, a man of few words."

"Take it or leave it." Even though it's summer, she's wearing an oversize sweater with sleeves so long they seem to swallow her fingers, and still she hunkers down within it, shivering.

"Guess I'll take it." She smiles in mocking fashion, displaying between her teeth a wad of gum. "Like I have a choice."

"So how are you?" he asks, not merely to be polite. He's curious to hear what she'll come up with.

"You can tell Kathleen I'm fine," she says shortly. Her tone is aggressive, and Tom battles an impulse to tell her to go to hell. But then she takes her display of impudence one step further and, mimicking a silly smile, chewing loudly, leans toward him and asks, "And how are you?"

Tom picks up the cigarette, taps the table with it, lets it drop.

"You're right. Enough bullshit. What was I thinking?"

He sometimes wonders how they reached this impasse, how these battle lines came to be drawn, because he doesn't dislike her and is honestly concerned for her welfare. Three years ago she was clean and sober, employed and engaged to be married to a law student, a young man in a shirt and tie with a gratingly earnest manner but possessing an appealing wholesomeness, if not a lot of worldly assets. Tom helped with their bills, set them up in a decent apartment, filled their refrigerator with food. Kathleen joined in on the wedding plans and introduced Beverly to her friends. Those are the days he wants to remember, when he and Beverly sat down and he listened while she talked about the mistakes she'd made and how she could never let down her guard because temptation was around every corner and she was at constant risk of slipping back. Her honesty and the ease with which she admitted her failings amazed him. And he talked too, opened himself up to the only person left in the world with whom he could share memories of his childhood. Then without warning her phone was disconnected and the young man was gone, and Beverly was calling in the middle of the night from the police station, where she'd been detained for public drunkenness. For whatever reason, the urge to cause damage had won out over whatever had prompted her toward kindness and stability. It's as if some perverse darkness governs her being. And he doesn't want this darkness contaminating his life. And especially not the lives of Kathleen and the kids.

"C'mon," she says, holding out her hand palm up, wiggling her fingers but gazing absent-mindedly out of the window instead of at him. "Hand over the goods."

Wearily, like a victim of extortion, he reaches into his shirt pocket and extracts a small envelope, folded over, containing five hundred dollars. From another pocket he retrieves the pack of cigarettes, Du Maurier Extra Light King Size. He flips these on the table, well away from her outstretched hand.

She snatches them up. "Thanks big brother," she says, pushing the cigarettes and the envelope into the gaping mouth of a black string bag.

"You getting something to eat?"

She smiles. "I should, shouldn't I? Since you're paying."

He signals to the waitress. Beverly orders eggs and bacon, toast and coffee. Tom refreshes his own coffee and orders fish and chips.

"So, how's the methadone treatment going?"

She tilts her head and, mockingly, widens her eyes. "So, how's your life going?"

Tom exhales deeply. "Here's an idea. Why don't we just sit and talk? I'm sick of fighting about nothing."

"*Nothing* is right. What the fuck do we have to fight about? I can't imagine."

"You know Bev," he says, his tone softening, "I'm not a bottomless pit. Someday I'll have nothing left to give to you. What are you going to do then? Where will you go?"

"Let me worry about that, why don't you?"

It's the attitude that gets to him: the arrogant smirk, the snooty insolence — the infantile suggestion of *Don't bug me I'll get around to it* in her tone, as if the world and all its treasures lie at her feet but right now she's too busy to bend over and pick them up.

"I guess I just don't understand why none of this makes any difference to you. Your life is a mess and you look like hell, and all you can do is dig yourself a deeper hole."

"As if you care," she says and stares fixedly at him, her eyes angry. But there's no hostility in her voice.

"Maybe I do care," he says, unwisely, because he knows it leaves him open to attack.

She leans over the table and smiles. "Well, as long as you're stupid enough to care, then I have nothing to worry about, do I? You'll always be there to bail me out."

"But what about when I stop caring?"

She smiles again. "Well, then I guess we'll be even."

He retreats into silence, taking grim pleasure from handling the cigarette, which is once again between his fingers, imagining how the bitter heat and pungency of smouldering tobacco will make its downward passage into his lungs when he gets outside. There is no denying that she got a raw deal, that her childhood was more than simply painful, and that she has a right to bear a grudge against anyone who knew she was suffering and did nothing about it. But why does she have to exult in the wrongs that were done to her? Why does she have to make everyone else suffer, even those who are trying to help her?

"You're high, aren't you?"

She cocks her eyebrows and allows a faint smile to hover around her lips. "I am what I am."

"My God, Beverly. If I can spot it this easy, how are you going to hide it from the people at the clinic? You'll get yourself kicked out again."

"Oh, now there's a worry."

He shakes his head but catches himself because he knows how it looks. He decides to take the conversation in another direction.

"I went to visit Mom last week."

Beverly gives no indication she's heard him. Her attention has shifted across the street, where cars are entering and leaving the parking lot of a grocery store. She chews her gum. Her fingers, intertwined on the table, tap out a twitchy, irregular rhythm.

"They're thinking of starting her on some new medication. It's supposed to make her more alert and interested in what's going on around her. Dr. Canfield hopes there might be some improvement."

Beverly rolls her eyes. Her lips move and she says something under her breath. The only word he catches is *fuck*.

"What?"

She turns to him, her mouth puckered with irritation. "I guess this is the price I have to pay, isn't it. The cost of doing business. Listening to a goddamn lecture and your stupid news from home." She gives the drawstring around the mouth of her purse a fierce tug. "God, you're a bore. You think I'm fucked up. Jesus, look at yourself. Maybe my life is a mess, but at least I've got a life. You've got nothing. You're a fucking slave, and you're so fucking dumb you don't even know the difference." She laughs sharply. "My brother, the dumb animal. Next time you expect me to sit through more of this shit, make it six hundred. Or a thousand. Yeah, next time why not make it a thousand?"

When the waitress returns with their orders they are not speaking and not looking at each other. Catching the mood of the table, she sets the plates down and swivels nimbly on her heel to make her escape.

Tom calls her back.

"Yes?"

"Can you add that up for me? I'll pay now. I've got to get back soon. Bev, you want anything else?"

Beverly raises her head and smiles sweetly. "Could you make me a chicken sandwich or something? Please? And coffee? To go?"

The waitress does a quick calculation and gives Tom a figure. He retrieves his wallet and counts out the money, adds a tip, and places the entire sum in her hand. He has to do it this way. Beverly will pocket any money left on the table.

Their silence continues as they tackle their meals. He eats quickly, but having lost much of his appetite, slides the rest of his lunch over to Beverly's plate. Delaying his departure for a moment to watch her eat, he picks up the cigarette again and cradles it in his hand, anticipating the moment when he can light up. Beverly finishes her toast and without breaking rhythm starts in on the fish and chips. But then she pauses and rolls up the sleeves of her sweater, revealing a row of puncture marks on her skinny forearm. She doesn't glance at him as she starts eating again, doesn't care what he sees. He recognizes the gesture for what it is: a deliberate attempt to shock or provoke or disgust him. But he's seen it all before. The only thing that startles him is discovering that he can almost comprehend his sister's compulsion to destroy herself: it's the only effective means of revenge at her disposal. He knows the money he's given her will be spent on drugs and booze, but even so a pang of tenderness halts his breath at the sight of her hungrily consuming a meal that he has provided. She's like a child, unable to provide for herself but ready, even as she denies her need, to snap up whatever crumbs fall within reach. Maybe this childlike vulnerability is what prompts the voice that whispers: it's not too late. You can bring her back. Something of this wreckage can be salvaged.

SIX

KATHLEEN'S FATHER OWNS a seaside cottage just outside a town called Wallace, on the province's northern shore. Tom began visiting there with Kathleen even before they were married. They've been so often that Tom sometimes claims he could make the trip in his sleep. Today, because he slept so poorly the previous night, he wonders if he will have to.

As he loads pieces of luggage and enough supplies for the week into the back of the van, and arranges a nest for the dog out of an old quilt, the headache that came on this morning stubbornly refuses to lift. Lately he finds himself plagued by a dampening of the spirits; he's not been himself, and Kathleen has informed him that he's "moody." His attention wanders at inopportune moments — while driving, while doing yet another brake job or while arguing with one of the younger mechanics about the inefficiencies of automatic transmissions. In just the past week he's snapped unkindly at both his children for trifling infractions, but it's young Charlie who gets on his nerves and receives the brunt of his irritation.

The boy is developing a deceitful manner and a whiny tone and lurks about the house with the sneaky furtiveness of a burglar. Sometimes Tom feels himself being watched, and even if he can't see anybody he knows the boy is close by. Occasionally, at the edge of his vision there is rapid movement and he hears a sound like the beating of wings, and he suspects the boy of spying. It has taken him years to organize his basement workroom and acquire all the tools he needs for the odd projects and repair jobs that come his way. He regards this space not only as private, but restricted as well. He has told his children they are not to venture there under any circumstances. But twice now he's found things moved or out of place. Once he was almost certain the table saw had been plugged in and switched on in his absence. It's an act of brazen defiance, a danger, and a challenge to his authority, and he has resolved to catch the boy in the act.

There's also a chance he's been drinking too much, but for now it's under control. After seeing what it did to his father, he has no desire to follow the old man down that path. But alcohol does bring a certain solace. After a few snorts of rye his equilibrium is restored. The heaviness of heart that weighs upon him lifts and disperses like fog dissolving under the heat of an early morning sun, and he can regard the approaching days and weeks with the uncluttered vision of a prophet. Under the consoling influence of alcohol his entire body shudders with relief, and he feels its thanks in the release of pressures and loosening of muscles. The bleak and barren distances that separate him from the rest of humanity vanish, replaced by the sparkling optimism and warm-hearted benevolence of a very fortunate man, one who can recognize his accomplishments for what they are and congratulate himself for how far he's come in just over twenty years.

The late June sun warms his back as he loads the van. Sammy scampers across the yard in pursuit of birds and dead leaves, stopping briefly to let Tom ruffle his ears. One of Tom's neighbours drives by, but there's no friendly acknowledgement and Tom concentrates on his task. He keeps himself to himself. Kathleen has met most of the families who live nearby and knows the children by name, but Tom would rather construct a ten-foot wall around the entire yard than engage in idle chat with people to whom he has nothing to say.

Kathleen is beside him. He hasn't even heard her approach.

"Sorry. This has to go in too." She hands him a blue duffel bag, stuffed full.

He emerges from his ruminations into a world of minor annoyances and feels the lines around his mouth harden. "Oh, yeah. Sure. No problem."

"I know, I know. It's my fault. Please, just see if you can find room for it." She turns to go. "Oh, Tom, did you remember the tools?"

It comes back to him now. He shakes his head. "I'll get them."

Silently he follows Kathleen into the house. As he descends the stairs to the basement his back stiffens at the sound of young Charlie wailing. It's always something with that boy, some nameless torment, some inconsolable grief, as if at the age of five he's already glimpsed the cruel disenchantments of middle age. Hannah, with the hushed and gentle nature of a penitent, uncomplainingly accepts whatever comes her way.

Kathleen's father has asked Tom to help him rebuild the porch of the cottage. For years the small timber-frame house has suffered from creeping rot, which, accelerated by ants and the salt air, has apparently claimed the porch as its first victim. Someday soon it's going to take a major investment to keep the building habitable, but for now they've settled on propping up the porch and replacing the rotten timbers. Tom enjoys Kathleen's father, Martin, a man much like himself, who can spend whole afternoons in the company of another human being without uttering a word. Martin has a few hand tools and will provide the necessary materials; Tom will bring his power tools. Together they can finish the job in a couple of days while Kathleen and the children swim and play on the beach.

Charlie's wailing rises in pitch and volume, becoming a scream that bores into Tom's brain. He clenches his jaw against the racket as he places the circular saw, jigsaw, router, drill, and extension cord into the tool bin. Suddenly it is quiet. He lets out a breath he hasn't realized he's been holding, grabs his tool belt and drapes it over his shoulder. The basement is cold in winter and damp the rest of the year. Mostly they use it for storage. But his workroom — separated from the rest of the basement by walls he built himself — is orderly and well lit; the concrete floor is spotless. As he surveys the only space in the house that he's been able to claim as his own, his chest swells with pride. Then the boy is wailing again, and the aching in his head is like an iron rod piercing his skull. Shadows close in around him. He's about to lift the bin and carry it upstairs when he turns, as if beckoned by a familiar voice. He puts the tool belt aside, then crouches and drags an old trunk from under the work table. Swinging back the lid, he gropes beneath a jumble of coloured rags and retrieves a half-empty bottle of Bonded Stock. He glances over his shoulder, unscrews the cap, raises the bottle to his lips. The amber fluid, dormant and benign in its container, erupts into fiery life as it rolls down his throat and into his belly. Immediately the muscles in his neck relax and the headache eases. He absorbs the benignity of the liquor, takes its sweetness into his soul. The heaviness that has stiffened his joints from the moment he woke this morning, that made his every movement a chore, vanishes. His brain clears. The irritableness is gone.

Much too soon and without warning, the bottle is empty. He stares at it, perplexed, as if the emptiness constitutes an accusation. He tucks the bottle quickly out of sight beneath the rags, closes the lid and pushes the trunk back into position. The child is still screeching, but this is no longer a concern. He hoists the bin filled with tools into his arms and lugs it up the stairs and outside, no lurch to his step, his hands steady as stone. Hannah is already in the van. She lifts her eyes

97

from the book she is reading long enough to exchange a smile with her father through the window. But her smile vanishes, and then there is another problem. He didn't trip or lose his balance, but somehow the bin is on the ground. The tools have spilled across the lawn and he's kneeling on the grass, trying to raise himself to his feet. He gets one foot under him and pushes himself upright, but then he's down again, this time on his back. The laughter he hears is his own. Something is very funny and he's trying to remember what it is so he can tell Kathleen about it.

But before he can recall the source of his amusement, Kathleen's voice reaches him, and he realizes it's what she's been saying that has struck him as hilarious.

"I can't believe it! You're drunk! It's not even nine in the morning and you're drunk!"

He hears his own voice bellow a response. "I'm not drunk. I'm not.... Don't you dare...."

"You're drunk, Tom! God!"

But then there's a gap, and he only comes to when the door slams and the engine starts. He raises himself, leaning on his elbows. She backs the van way too fast down the driveway and squeals the tires when she shifts gears. Sitting up now, Tom watches through tears of laughter as his family drives away — even the dog is abandoning him — and is still laughing when the van turns the corner and disappears from view. All of it strikes him as uproariously comical because he simply cannot imagine where she thinks she's going without him.

A WEEK LATER, in a teary phone call from the cottage, Kathleen demands his sobriety. He responds earnestly, swearing he understands that if he touches alcohol again he will find himself in deep trouble. Already he's taken a first step. Not trusting himself to pour the booze down the drain, he called Kenny Harrow from work to come and take it away, pointing out all the hidden bottles. Since then he has filled his time with errands: cleaning the house and tidying the yard, mowing the grass, straightening things in the attic, organizing his tools. Every morning he gets up early and takes the bus to work. To escape the house in the evening he walks around the neighborhood as if walking the dog, sometimes staying out until after dark, thinking the exercise can't do him any harm. None of the neighbours come near him. Those he sees avoid eye contact. Though his memory of the incident is fuzzy, he's almost certain a couple of people were outside when Kathleen yelled at him and drove off, leaving him flat on his ass laughing his head off like a damn fool. Word gets around. The humiliation grinds away at him, but he tries to be thankful because the only way he was going to stop drinking was to get caught. And he was lucky enough to get caught before it finished him off.

A month after the phone call Kathleen returns with the children. He tries to control himself, but he's overjoyed, jittery with hope that everything will get back to normal. He can't wait to hug his children and ruffle Sammy's ears. He can't wait for Kathleen to see how clean the house is. He can't wait to tell her he's been sober for five weeks. But everyone is tired,

IAN COLFORD

the children reserved and standoffish, especially Hannah. Her
coolness toward him nearly breaks his heart. He offers to get
Kentucky Fried Chicken for supper — a special treat — but no one
will come with him, so he goes by himself to pick up the food.
They eat quietly in the kitchen and the children go to bed early.

"I'm so glad you're back," he tells Kathleen in bed after
they've made love. He tries to apologize again, but only gets as
far as "I'm sorry," before she touches his lips with her fingertip
and whispers, "Shhhh. Let's not do that anymore."

They snuggle down and go to sleep. But later in the night
Tom wakes to the sound of childish laughter and whispering.
He leaves Kathleen in bed and creeps through the house, top
to bottom, but everything is in order. Hannah and Charlie
are asleep in their rooms. Sammy's on his cushion. But now
Tom's fully awake, and he hears that sound again: a whirring,
like the beating of wings. He goes into the bathroom and sits
on the toilet with his face in his hands. A few minutes later
he startles himself awake. He gets up and turns on the light.
The face in the mirror stares back at him with his mother's
and his father's eyes.

The darkness descends.

"YOU MIGHT WANT to think about getting some help, Tom."

Kathleen sets his coffee on the table. It is six months later.
Another Christmas has just passed and Hannah and Charlie are
outside on this bright Saturday morning in January playing in
the new snow. The radio in the background is set to Country 101.

Her statement does not altogether catch him by surprise. His mood swings have come upon him with alarming suddenness lately. All it takes is a word from someone, and for no reason his jaw tenses and he's struggling to choke back an answer he'll regret. He's sensed her concern for weeks, watched her watching him with a sombre singleness of purpose that makes him uncomfortable and even more determined to pretend that all is well. This morning he might have seen the remark coming, if he'd even once looked into her eyes.

"Help? What are you talking about?"

"I think you know. It's not easy to say this, but I don't think you're very happy. I don't know if you try to hide it or not, but it's there for anyone to see."

"Kathleen, lighten up. Okay? Just because I'm not singing and dancing doesn't mean I'm not happy." He searches her face and shrugs. "It's just the way I am. I'm a serious guy. I thought you'd be used to it by now."

She slides her hand across the table and he accepts it. It's their first physical contact in several days.

"Tom, I can tell it's more than that. It's in your eyes and the way you do things and how you move. You're tired and you're sad and I get the feeling that whatever's eating you is going to take you away from me."

He laughs. "That's ridiculous. You're saying I should go to a shrink? Why, for God's sake?"

"You never spoke to anyone about the alcoholism, did you?"

"I didn't have to."

"But, that kind of thing.... Considering what it did to your family. How can you just go on pretending nothing happened?"

"I'm not 'pretending' anything. I know what happened, and I know if I'm not careful it could happen again. What good would it do to tell all that to a complete stranger?"

"But talking about things is good," she says. "You'd be surprised how light it makes you feel, just to share your troubles with someone else."

"I've never been much of a talker," he jokes and is then gladdened by her smile. "Seriously, no one can tell me anything I don't already know."

He is struck by how lovely she is this morning, seated across from him, the winter sunlight ablaze in her hair. Her skin has retained a youthful radiance, and even after bearing two children her body remains slim and firm, her muscles taut. She closes her eyes and allows him to stroke her cheek. He is so grateful to her, not least for helping him to see, when both his sister and his father dropped out of his life, that it was not his fault, that adults make choices and eventually you have to stop chasing after them and offering help they don't want. Right now though, he doesn't want her help, because the truth frightens him and he lacks the faith and courage to look it in the eye. What he wants is distraction, an end to the questions. He leads her upstairs to the bedroom, but even as he buries himself in her, he cannot erase from his mind the face in the mirror, nor shut his ears to the beating of wings.

SEVEN

FOR THE FIRST TIME in his life Tom has been reprimanded at work. The new manager of the service station, a kid with a college degree but no experience, summoned him into the office and reminded him that recent changes in policy mean that customer relations are everything.

"I don't care how good you are," the kid says with a magisterial wave of his hand, "if your attitude sucks and you piss people off, you're gone." He stares at Tom with that thin-lipped cheekiness he's perfected since taking over from Clyde the previous year. His name is Mack, short for something or other, Tom can't remember what. Because his thin, reedy voice chafes Tom's eardrums, Tom usually tunes it out. Mack reclines in his chair and links his hands behind his head. He's a runt, but Tom imagines he was a bully in school, terrorizing the smaller kids and throwing rocks at cats and dogs.

"Twenty years' service don't count for much these days, huh kid."

"Look, Brackett," Mack says, then moderates his tone, "Tom, I know you're the best mechanic here. But when you tell some guy to go fuck himself, it doesn't do anyone any good and I take shit for it."

Tom grins at the memory, the old bastard with the second-hand Lincoln he just bought that needed a whole new transmission. The thing was shot and the guy's going around telling people he's being ripped off. A guy with a Lincoln, even a second-hand one, can afford a new transmission.

"Customer's always right I guess."

"Well, I hope you remember those comment cards aren't there so you can wipe your ass with them. I take any more heat on your account, you can call it a day."

Tom pulls a tissue from the box on Mack's desk and blows his nose.

"Anything else?"

From Mack's office he goes outside for a smoke. Kenny nods a greeting but when Tom growls, "Fucking little asshole, thinks he's God's gift," Kenny says nothing, won't meet his eye, just glances at the ground, scuffs his boot in the gravel and coughs lightly. It makes Tom feel strange, like he's violated some code he didn't even know existed. He stubs out his half-smoked cigarette, goes back in and starts looking over Dr. Brimmer's malfunctioning torque converter, but when he sees that his hands are trembling, he decides to knock off early.

Driving home in the old Land Rover he recently bought for his own use, he tries to quell the competing voices in his head, one telling him the old guy had it coming, the other asking why he's doing stupid things that could cost him his job. Lately he feels he's drowning in a sea of voices: a whispering, crying, and howling chorus so persistent he can't find his own thoughts in all that clamour.

It's March and spring has finally breached the wintry surface of things with its mixed promise of renewal and decay. The roads and the sky are clear. Walking with Sammy last week in the pine forest out near Half Mile Lake, he came across the rotting carcass of a deer newly exposed by the retreating blanket of snow. Sammy sniffed at it, whined, and pawed at the dirt, and then looked mournfully to Tom. The animal bore no traces of having been shot. Its dead eyes, open and blank, seemed eerily attentive to Tom's movements. Its tawny fur had lost its sheen, but even so Tom had to still an impulse to reach down and lay his hand on it. Maybe it had become separated from the herd in a storm and lost its way. Set upon by howling winds and swirling snow and seeing no way out, had it panicked and run, or just curled up and waited, as who knows what fears and yearnings passed through its consciousness? He wondered if animals look back on their lives as humans do, remembering particular moments with pleasure or bitterness or regret. Suddenly Sammy was barking and he realized he had travelled far from the deer and the forest and down some twisted pathway in his mind, toward a deepening twilight of the self. Tom kicked loose snow and earth over the carcass and continued on his way. How long had he been standing over the dead animal? The air had left him chilled and the sun's light was quickly fading.

When he pulls into the driveway it's half past three. The van is there. Kathleen and the children are probably at home. His throat muscles tighten with the suspicion that none of them are eager to have him stifle their lives with his brooding presence.

He enters by the side door, hangs up his jacket and exchanges his work boots for a pair of well-worn leather loafers. The house is immersed in a depthless mid-afternoon silence. Maybe Kathleen's napping. Maybe they're all napping. Where's Sammy, he wonders, because usually the dog is there when he arrives, leaping and going in circles, begging to be walked. He treads carefully through the kitchen and into the living room. Sunlight angles steeply through the window, casting an oblong of light on the carpet. It's eerily peaceful, the air so still he can see dust floating. But the quiet is unsettling and reminds him that nobody is expecting him to be here this early. It's not his intention to surprise anyone or disturb the silence, but he can't help wondering where they are and what they're up to.

Back in the kitchen he hears a distant whirring sound and holds himself still in mid-stride. The whirring stops, starts up again. Stops. Lurking beneath the silence is whispering, childish laughter, giggling. He clenches his jaw. The door leading to the basement is closed, but when he gently pulls it open he sees the lights are on. He descends cautiously and somehow, as if blessed, the stairs fail to emit their customary creaks and groans under his weight. The door to his workshop is barely ajar but from behind it he hears the unmistakable buzzing of the table saw. It continues for a moment and then is switched off. Then it's on again. Then off. Then on. He crosses the concrete floor, eases the door open and peers through the crack. Charlie's standing by the saw, his back to Tom, one finger poised above the power switch. Sammy's lying on the floor. Charlie says, "This is how it works, Sammy. See?" He turns the saw on, then off. "See?" Tom flings the door open so hard it bangs against the corner of the work table. Sammy jumps up and wags his tail, looking like he's smiling. But when Charlie turns to face his father Sammy starts to whimper. The saw is off. But Tom can still hear the whirring, like the beating of wings, so loud now it almost drowns out the voices. Tom has to raise his own voice to hear himself above all the noise.

"What are you doing in here?"

His son backs away. The boy's features are frozen. His eyes are wide open and shining with liquid.

"Don't be a dumbass. I asked you what you're doing in here."

"I don't know."

"You don't know what you're doing in here?" Tom pauses. "Are you supposed to be in here? Did someone tell you to come in here?"

Charlie shakes his head and doesn't take his eyes from Tom's.

"I asked you not to come in here, didn't I?"

Charlie nods, still backing away as Tom draws near.

"Speak up."

"Yes, sir."

"So, you're in here even though I asked you not to come in here. Is that right?"

"Yes, sir."

"What were you doing in here? Were you playing with the table saw?"

"No, sir."

Charlie's back is up against a set of metal shelves. He can't go any further. He draws a sobbing breath. Tom's surprised he can still hear the boy over the pounding of his heart and the tumult of voices and the beating, whirring sounds that seem to emanate from the walls.

"I heard you switching it on and off. So now I'll ask again. Were you playing with the table saw?"

"Yes, sir."

"Do you know how dangerous that is?"

"Yes, sir."

And then it's as if he's been lifted out of himself and is looking down on the scene from above. Charlie's small chest rises and falls with each intake of breath. Tom's hand reaches out to grip his son's arm.

"I don't think you do know," he hears himself say. "I think I have to show you."

Tom drags his son across the floor but the boy pulls his arm free and scrambles backward until once again he comes up against the metal shelves. Tom has him cornered. Charlie sinks to the floor and covers his head with his arms.

"Daddy, no! I'm sorry."

Tom yanks him to his feet. Charlie makes a grab for the shelf but Tom jerks him out of range.

Now they are both standing beside the saw, Tom's big right hand grasping the boy by the left wrist. Charlie is shaking and sobbing but no longer struggling.

"Turn it on," Tom commands. "I know you know how to do it."

Keeping both eyes forward, Charlie moves his free hand to the switch, which is protected by a plastic flap. With his small fingers he folds the piece of plastic up and presses the switch. The machine springs smoothly to life. The blade spins, emitting a steady hum.

"That blade," Tom says, indicating the moving metal disk just visible beneath its shield, "is going around a thousand times a minute. It doesn't matter what I put in there —" He takes a small block of scrap pine from the work table, butts it up against the rail, and with his left hand pushes it lengthwise toward the blade. "It'll rip right through it."

The rotating blade opens a gash in the wood, the ugly whine almost drowning out the chorus of voices screaming in Tom's head. He's off balance, holding the wood awkwardly and not wearing goggles, but he feels immune to the danger. Shavings collect on the platform and ascend lightly into the still air. The saw shoots out a splinter of wood and Charlie

flinches and raises his arm to cover his face. The remnant
Tom was holding slips from his fingers. The dog is barking.
Charlie is shrieking and struggling to free himself. From a
great distance Tom looks down on the scene of a man forcing
a boy's hand toward a rotating blade. But he's too far away to
stop what's happening. The blade's whine grows louder and
there's blood and a scattering of shredded bone and tissue
and it's like he's watching a film with a faulty soundtrack —
even when Kathleen appears and scoops up Charlie's crumpled
body, her features distorted with horror and fear, and he can
see she's making sounds with her mouth, even then he hears
nothing but the drone of the rotating blade.

After a few moments it occurs to him to shut off the saw's
power. Though its hum calms his heart and brain, he needs
to conserve its motor. But the sight of blood on the platform
makes him pause. There is also blood on the floor, blood on his
shirt and trousers. He follows the trail of blood up the stairs
to the kitchen. Here the blood has pooled in the centre of the
floor. Several drawers and cupboard doors have been opened
and left that way, as if someone has conducted a frenzied
search. Bloody footprints lead from the kitchen to the living
room and out to the front steps. Tire tracks gouge the lawn
where Kathleen drove the van in order to get past the Rover.

The air is cool. He searches his pockets for a cigarette
and matches and then remembers they are in his jacket. He
goes back in, retrieves his jacket from the closet, then, as if
preparing for a journey, removes his blood-spattered loafers

and pulls on his boots. He forgets the cigarette for the moment and, because it's suppertime, begins searching for food. There is a package of four pork chops in the refrigerator. He finds a frying pan, and with some butter and salt and pepper, begins frying all four. Somewhere along the way it occurs to him that he might have forgotten to switch off the saw, but his mind drifts away from the question and he doesn't think of it again. When the chops are fried up the way he likes them — the surface dark brown, the fatty edges crisp — he lifts the pan off the burner and carries the whole thing to the table, stepping carefully to avoid the blood. He gets a knife and fork from the drawer and eats the four chops straight out of the pan.

When he's finished he dumps the bones in the garbage and leaves the greasy frying pan in the sink. Then he goes through the living room and out the front door. It's after six o'clock. The light is beginning to dim. As he gazes absently toward the sky thin tendrils of cloud take on surreal hues of orange and pink. Sitting down on the steps, he lights a cigarette. The yard is a mess, full of stones heaved up by the frosts of winters past, wind-strewn garbage, and fermenting dog turds left behind by the retreating snow. The grass is patchy, weedy, and unwholesome. A few years back Kathleen planted some evergreen shrubs, but something in the soil, or maybe it was the harsh winters or the wrong exposure, kept them from thriving. Shapeless and forlorn in the failing evening light, scorched by a succession of unforgiving summer suns, the juniper and miniature cedar, hydrangea, and holly bush resemble bent-backed refugees from some borderland racked by armed conflict.

A car drives by. He follows it until it rounds a turn and disappears up another street. There's new construction going on at that end of the neighbourhood. Every day the crews take down more trees, dig more foundations. It never stops. Since they moved in the development has doubled in size. More houses, more cars, more people. His gaze falls on the house across the street, so close it seems to loom over him. He notices the curtains in the front window moving. Someone is standing there. He can see the outline of a figure but can't make out who it is, the light is too dim, but he feels eyes on him. And with the sudden insight of a man who has finally glimpsed the source of a puzzling discontent, he understands that he was never meant to live in cramped quarters like this, in a place where there's no breathing room between houses. He should have moved his family out of town to some rural community where there's lots of space, where you're not looking out of your own window and into the window of the house next door, where you're not forced to mix with folks just because you can't get yourself clear of the sight of them.

He taps the ash from the cigarette. The evening is cooling, the sun setting quickly. The air around him moves and a refreshing chill embraces him. He likes being alone. There's nobody talking at him, telling him to do things. This is the first chance he's had all day to relax. But then Mack's whiny voice comes into his head telling him his attitude sucks, and his neck stiffens with fury. He crushes the cigarette out on the step and lights another. Someone should teach that little prick a lesson. It comes to him that if he went in there with a gun Mack would be a sitting duck. He grins at the thought, the image of that asshole on his knees begging for his life. He wouldn't shoot him, though, just scare the living shit right out of him. But if he did want to shoot him there's no way the guy would get away. If only he had a gun. And then he remembers he does have a gun, an old 12-gauge shotgun he got years ago from somebody, some salesman or farmhand with no money, whose car he fixed right after he started working at the Shell station. He's been carting the thing around for twenty years now, renewing his acquaintance with it whenever he had to pack up and move from one place to another. Never used it, not once, not even to go hunting.

He's on his feet and about to return to the basement and get the gun down from its hiding place in the ceiling joists when a police car rolls around the corner and pulls up in front of the house. And with another dizzying flash of insight, he realizes he's been expecting this, or something like it. All evening he's been waiting for a sign that Kathleen has set the process of revenge in motion.

Just like on TV, there's a heavy old one and a skinny young one. They set their hats in place as they climb slowly out of the cruiser. They both have those slim black clubs dangling from their belts. They say a few words to each other and an uneasy smile spreads across the face of the young one.

Tom draws the jacket closed over his blood-spattered shirt and takes a few steps toward them as they approach, standing behind a bush so they can't see his pants.

"Evening, officer," he says cordially, as the older of the two uniformed men comes up the walkway, the younger one hanging back at the edge of the property. "Something the matter?"

"You Tom Brackett?"

"Yes, sir. That's me."

"There's been a report of a disturbance. Know anything about that?"

"A disturbance? My son hurt himself with the table saw. I'd call it an accident, not a disturbance."

The cop stares at him, apparently waiting for him to go on.

When Tom says nothing further the cop says, "Your wife claims it was no accident."

Tom tries to look confused. "What do you mean?"

"She says your boy says you hurt him on purpose, and she believes him."

Tom takes the cigarette from his mouth and flicks it away. He shakes his head.

"Well, officer. I don't know what to tell you. I just got in the door from working all day and first thing I hear is all this screaming and crying. I go downstairs and there's this mess, you know, blood everywhere. I been busy cleaning that up. I guess I forgot to lock the workroom and Charlie, my son, well he must've got in there and was playing with the saw.

Truth is I was too shaken up to drive, so Kathleen took him in. But I'm heading to the hospital in a few minutes."

The policeman reaches his hand up beneath his hat and scratches his head. Even in weak light the weariness in his puffy eyes is plain to see.

"It's one hell of an injury for a boy to do to himself. His hand's almost cut in half, from the knuckle clean through to the wrist."

"Did you see him? Is he doing okay?"

"We talked to the doctor and your wife. The boy's sedated. It's going to be a major operation, stitching it back together. They don't know if he'll ever be able to use it again."

"Fuck. You know, I told him over and over not to go in there." Tom rubs his eyes. "You got kids, officer?" The policeman makes no response and Tom goes on. The situation has him oddly elated, juiced up. Strangely, he doesn't feel the least bit nervous. "It's a big fucking responsibility, let me tell you. Just keeping them out of harm's way — shit, that'll keep you busy day and night. It's not an easy thing, raising kids. It doesn't matter what you do, they'll find trouble, or trouble'll find them. It happens. And kids lie. All the time, 'specially if they think you're going to get mad at them for something. You know what I'm saying? With Charlie, well, him telling lies has been a problem. We're trying to figure out what to do about it."

In the silence that follows he senses the man weighing his words, waiting, perhaps, to be convinced.

"So you're saying the boy did this to himself and then lied about what happened to his mother so he wouldn't get into trouble."

"Yes, sir. He was on the floor wailing when I got there. I couldn't believe what I was seeing."

The cop writes something in a notebook that Tom hadn't even noticed was in his hand.

They are now enveloped by the advancing gloom. As the man relaxes his posture and jots his notes, Tom realizes the version of events he has just described makes more sense than what Charlie or Kathleen have told them. The cops have to accept his story because the alternative is to believe that a man deliberately fed his son's hand into a table saw.

Then a streetlamp crackles and sprays a cone of silver light, illuminating the cruiser and the younger police officer where he stands, arms crossed, at the property line.

"We'll come in and take a look around, if that's alright with you."

Tom stares hard at the cop, trying to get the measure of his mood, but the man's expression reveals nothing. The young one comes up the path and Tom leads them into the house. It's dark now and he switches on the lights so they can see where they're going. They walk through the living room and into the kitchen, where the puddle of blood is dry at the edges. The bloody footprints are vivid burgundy stains against the white tile floor. The kitchen smells of grease and for a second they all stare at the dirty frying pan in the sink, and at the drawers and cupboard doors that are still open. Nobody says anything. Tom leads them down the stairs to the basement. The saw is off. Some rags have fallen from the shelf to the floor, making it look like a clean-up is in progress. The young cop pulls out a flashlight and shines the beam around, on the saw covered with blood and wood shavings, on the bloody floor, into various corners of the room, and finally on Tom, illuminating the patches of blood on his pants.

Tom shrugs. "It's like I said."

"Mr. Brackett, was there a fight?" It's the young cop asking.

"A fight?"

"Did you fight with your son or your wife?"

This time Tom doesn't have to feign confusion. "Who said there was a fight?"

"Please answer the question."

Tom shakes his head. "No, sir. There was no fight."

The cops roam through the workroom for another couple of minutes, their eyes alert.

Then the old one says, "Okay, we're finished here."

Tom leads them up the stairs. Nobody says anything. Tom's heart is pounding and something niggles away at him. There's some detail he's forgotten. And he doesn't like the two cops bringing up the rear, where he can't see them. He hears them whispering, but can't make out what they're saying.

They go out to the front of the house. The sky is completely dark and there are lights on in the surrounding houses. The cruiser gleams beneath the light of the streetlamp.

The old one says, "Just sit tight, now. We're going to radio in."

Tom watches them retrace their steps. Without realizing he's moved even a single muscle, he finds a cigarette in his hand. He lights it. The two policemen climb back into the cruiser, slamming the doors in unison. The young cop brings the radio to his mouth.

Tom drops the cigarette and goes inside. Except for the blood, everything appears normal in the living room. The furniture is not toppled; the framed photographs and ornamental figurines are not smashed and strewn about. Confusion descends on him like a shroud, smothering him, muddying the version of events that insists on playing and replaying itself in his mind. What's missing is an answer, a reason why all this is happening. He's not going to find it in the kitchen, but that's where he goes. He stares at the blood. At the mess in the sink. The noise he'd thought was the cops whispering is still there, even though they're outside. It sounds far away and close by at the same time.

Something resembling panic has begun shooting through his muscles, making them jump and squirm. Suddenly nothing looks familiar. He's afraid. He has no idea what to do next. Halfway down the stairs to the basement he forces himself to sit because he doesn't know what he's doing and realizes he won't get through this unless he can decipher his intentions every step of the way. He holds his head in his hands, hoping this will stop the whispering and snuff out the images that appear in his brain: his parents arguing, his mother in the bathtub, his sister sitting across from him in the restaurant eyeing him with a mixture of amusement and contempt as he counts out the cash, the long road to nowhere leading away from his grandmother's house. Charlie, struggling and screaming, his eyes ablaze with terror, Kathleen's face a mask of revulsion. For a single horrible instant the fog lifts, and he comprehends the harm he has caused. The tears he sheds are real. With something like disgust he listens to the sound he makes weeping for his ruined life. Then the curtain descends. The tears dry up and he watches through unfeeling eyes the spectacle of a grown man unable to cope with sorrow and disgrace.

EIGHT

IT TAKES A FEW MONTHS for Tom to accept that there will be no reconciliation with Kathleen. The realization dawns on him while he is undergoing treatment for depression and borderline personality disorder. During this period of his life, which he describes later as his private hell, he is haunted by nightmares. They are always the same, reaching their climax with his son's hand touching the blade and bursting open like a piece of ripe fruit, discharging a torrent of blood and bone and ripped tissue into Tom's face. And yet, on another level he continues to resist what Kathleen and his criminal record are constantly reminding him of: that he was capable of doing such a thing. Several times a day he will pause in the middle of some mundane task and, revising history, watch himself come up from behind and yank his son's hand away from the saw just as the rotating blade is about to start taking bites out of his son's flesh. Trembling and faint with gratitude, young Charlie gazes into his father's eyes before they embrace and go upstairs.

Tom was arrested and charged with assault. When the two cops came back into the house they found him crouched on the basement stairs engaged in argument with a variety of individuals present only in his head. He spent a night in jail before being transported to the Abbie J. Lane Hospital for a psychological evaluation. Months later his doctors are still adjusting his medication. He had heard the term schizophrenic used with regard to his mother, but even when the clamouring voices were at their loudest, even with the blackouts and the disembodied feeling that enabled him to push his son's hand into a rotary saw blade, he never once suspected that he was suffering from a version of the same illness.

His only communication with Kathleen is through a lawyer, a slender young man with a poker face and the anxious mannerisms of someone who has blundered into hostile territory and is seeking a furtive means of escape. The lawyer's name is Turcotte. He rarely looks Tom in the eye and is constantly fiddling with the collar of his shirt, prying it loose from his neck. Their meetings take place in a day room at the end of the corridor of the psych ward. Tom sits through them with his hands folded on the table and struggles to keep his mind from drifting. As Turcotte outlines Kathleen's demands, Tom nods solemnly and tries not to stare directly into the man's face for too long at a stretch, fearing this will make Turcotte more uncomfortable than he already is. Occasionally Tom senses that he should feel some degree of hostility toward this skinny young fellow in a suit, with his book learning and fancy words, who is taking his family away from him. But hostility never materializes. The only desire that stays with him is to understand, or to make a convincing show of understanding, everything he's being told so Turcotte won't feel his time is being wasted.

The drugs have defused his anger. They have levelled him, providing relief from the voices and the suspicions that people are sneaking around and whispering behind his back. A burden has been lifted, and with the mental weight gone he feels physically lighter. He suffers no dark thoughts. He sheds no tears when agreeing to stay away from his children and does not feel his gorge rise when Turcotte refers to Kathleen as his "former wife." Tom has no lawyer of his own and does not want one. Suffering no qualms, he signed a piece of paper stating his desire to act for himself and watched with benign satisfaction as Turcotte inserted it into a zippered compartment in his briefcase. He sits cosily in a drug-induced lethargy, vaguely aware that he has given his consent to conditions that will not benefit him in the long run. Maybe he should speak up. But today he has achieved balance. He feels right in the head. To make some clamorous objection would upset the precious equilibrium. In the end he wants only what is best for everyone and trusts Kathleen and Turcotte to figure out what that is.

The last documents are signed. Within a matter of weeks the divorce will be final. They shake hands and Turcotte leaves. Tom goes to the window and gazes down upon a city in which he is completely alone.

NINE

MOST WEEKENDS Tom rents a car and goes driving, purposely avoiding the road leading to the house, which, since he signed away his portion, now belongs to Kathleen. He has always wanted to walk on a beach in winter and down along the south shore he can take his pick.

The one he chooses today has no name that he can find — it is a barren scythe-shaped stretch of sandy soil at the end of a mile-long unpaved road. The road to the sea takes him past a scattering of small houses and cottages. Smoke meanders from chimneys. A larger, newer house sits on the crest of the last hill before the beach, but he has come this way several times and never seen any signs of habitation.

After a year Tom's tightly regulated life is loosening. Meetings with doctors that used to be weekly are now monthly. His conviction on assault charges resulted in a sentence of probation, but as long as he's taking his meds he only has to report in by phone. He has had no direct contact with Kathleen but keeps up through Turcotte. The reconstructive surgery on Charlie's hand is progressing in stages.

He leaves the rental car — this week it's a grey Toyota Echo, the cheapest thing on the lot — at the end of the road and walks with difficulty through the thick, scrubby undergrowth. It is cold for the last week of December. The frost-hardened sand is lightly powdered with snow, the sky a lucid crystalline blue you only see outside the city. He felt no wind getting out of the car, but as he approaches the surf the breeze off the water grows steady and stronger and whistles with a high-pitched howl. A lone gull hovers motionless above him, riding the wind. Near the water it is intensely cold. He grabs his cap just as a sudden gust pulls it from his head.

Habit is comforting. He understands this much about himself: he enjoys a routine. But despite his determination to walk today, he must admit the cold adds nothing pleasurable to the experience.

He slaps his hands together and huddles deeper into his coat. He decided early in his rehabilitation that he was not going to follow the family pattern and become a wreck. Of the many forms of therapy on offer, talking helped the most. When it dawned on him that blame for what happened was not necessarily a burden he had to shoulder alone, survival became an option. Later, when he left the halfway house to live in an apartment, it was with the understanding that several paths lay before him and it was up to him to choose. He could dive headlong into alcohol and drugs, saturate his body with poisons, and end up dead in a year or two; he could make a half-hearted attempt to stay sober and prolong a process that was going to cause pain for everyone he came into contact with; or he could build a new life out of the scraps that had been tossed his way.

It was not easy to find a place to live. His tiny second-floor walk-up barely qualifies as habitable. Part of a century-old neighbourhood across the street from Bloomfield School, the original house lies submerged beneath a rickety patchwork of add-on construction. The cardboard walls allow music and radio and television voices to filter from one apartment to the next. His only window faces the asphalt school grounds and his room suffers the fierce glare of twenty-four hour security lights. The second-hand furniture was there when he arrived. The only change he's made is to fill the single closet and the dresser drawers with his clothes. Tom does not seek out his neighbours, but meeting them is often unavoidable. Across the hall lives an elderly man with a stocky build, a red face, and sparse hair who always wears a grey sweater with holes at the elbows. When they encounter one another, they exchange a silent nod. Tom has paused on the landing outside the man's door — day or night, it doesn't seem to matter — and heard voices, or at any rate a single voice, whispering, as if in conversation. He's not imagining it. Sometimes he awakens to this whispering. It has no beginning and no end. He considers this home temporary.

His custodial job at the Park Lane Shopping Mall is not demanding. Often he volunteers for extra shifts and has told his supervisor that he's available when people call in sick.

He keeps himself in good shape. His physical endurance is formidable and he likes to test himself. He also wants to prove that he can be counted on. Eventually he will find a more challenging job — with luck, one that draws upon his twenty years of experience rebuilding car engines from the inside out — but for now he's content to mop floors at the mall and let his mind rummage through an accumulation of memories, good and bad. He buys warm clothes at a nearby used-clothing shop. He eats well. He keeps himself well groomed. Maybe he's sick and has to take pills for the rest of his life, but he doesn't have to let everyone who passes him on the street know it just by looking at him.

No cheating — he forces himself to walk the length of the beach. Driven by the wind, waves crash rhythmically, hypnotically, against the smoothly rounded outcropping of rock at the farthest end of the curve, the sharpened tip of the scythe. The spray catches him, but he stands and watches for a few moments, smelling the salt, as the skin of his face grows numb. He misses Sammy as much as he misses his wife and children — in some ways more — and he makes an idle promise to himself that before too many more months go by he'll come back to this beach with a dog.

The walk back to the car seems very long, but he doesn't want to hurry. Chilled through but in love with every breath that enters his lungs, he slams the car door and grabs his thermos of Tim Horton's coffee. The first sip scalds his throat. Tears flood his eyes, but this does nothing to dampen his enthusiasm for the outing. He starts the engine — despite being a piece of junk, the car has an efficient heater — and turns the heat all the way up. As the steam from the coffee dissipates he settles back and tries to identify the source of his euphoria. It cannot be the drugs, which, though calibrated to fight his depression, are not of a type to induce jubilation. In the past year he has learned a great deal about mental illnesses and the medications that treat them: the mind is like a car, responding to stimuli, functioning and malfunctioning in ways that are uniquely its own, and the doctors are like mechanics working on overly sensitive mechanisms that produce new symptoms for every remedy they try. It took months of tinkering with his drugs before they hit upon his own unique cocktail. Over the months, as one failed treatment followed another, he experienced a series of excruciating side-effects: insomnia, diarrhoea, bloating, uncontrollable trembling, hallucinations, pain in the extremities, double vision. He decided he was being punished for what he had done to Charlie, and the thought that he deserved to suffer in a way that turned his body against itself was one of the things that pulled him through to the other side. When the pain finally subsided and the crushing sadness lifted — when the voices urging him to do terrible things had fallen silent — it was as if the guards had all gone home, the prison had been abandoned and he was free to come and go as he pleased. He knows the drugs might stop working at any moment, but in the meantime he takes them willingly, even though they often give him cramps and cloak his brain in a numbing fog.

But sometimes a smell or a sound — the dark richness of hot coffee or the raucous laughter of children playing — cuts through the fog, giving him a moment of sharp clarity. Maybe this excess of happiness is his true nature. After years of anxiety and depression he's finally discovering what it means to be Tom Brackett.

Repeated tapping on the passenger-side window draws him out of his reverie. A woman wearing a red scarf and matching red leather gloves is looking at him.

"Hello?" Her voice through the glass is muffled.

He opens the door and climbs out. After the coffee the cold hits him hard.

"I'm sorry," she says, her tone formal and her enunciation vaguely accented. "You can't park here. It's private property."

"Hey, I'm sorry," he says, flustered, fumbling to wipe a dribble of coffee from his chin. "I didn't see a sign."

"You city people," she exclaims, her breath clouding the air. "If there's no sign you think you can do whatever you want." She shakes her head and flings her hand in irritation. The scarf, tied into a busy knot beneath her chin, does not completely hold in place a disorderly mop of black hair. Her eyes are deep hazel green and her skin unnaturally pale. She could be anywhere from thirty to fifty. She looks like someone who has been recently confined to a sickbed.

Then, to his surprise, she's tilting her head coquettishly and smiling. "What on earth are you doing out here? It's at least twenty below." Her voice loops and curls like she's singing a song.

"Just walking on the beach." He says nothing further, waiting, he realizes, for her to tell him he's got to be crazy. To which he can reply in all honesty, *Yes, I am.* Or perhaps, *Not as crazy as I used to be.* "It's not private too, is it?"

"Oh, no. They'll never let us buy the beach!" She shakes her head, and the exaggerated hand gesture that accompanies this statement tells him she's drunk. "Not that we haven't tried. Some stupid rule or other. You know how it is."

"Aren't you cold?" he asks, closing the door and stepping around the car. "Maybe it's time to get back inside."

"You'll move the car, won't you? Lester gets so mad."

The suggestion of familiarity in her manner makes him wonder if she's mistaken him for someone: a friend or hired hand. "You know I will," he says softly as he comes up to her.

She seems distracted now and touches the scarf with her fingers, trying to straighten her hair, which spills out from beneath it. What he'd thought was a cream-coloured winter jacket turns out to be a quilted housecoat. Inside fuzzy white slippers her feet are bare.

Without a word he takes her by the elbow.

"Who'll do the yard work?" she asks with a doleful glance in his direction as he gently directs her toward the house on the crest of the hill. But even as she gazes at him her eyes lose their focus and drift elsewhere.

"I don't think we need to worry about that today."

She doesn't resist his touch. Her steps are silent while his crunch heavily on the frozen earth.

"No, I suppose not," she agrees dreamily.

They approach the house along a gravel walkway bordered by pressure-treated two-by-fours; there is no driveway or garage. The house is alone at the end of the road, encroached upon by forest that obscures the neighbouring houses. The wooden front steps, painted grey but flaking, rest on a concrete slab. Through the lattice closing in the space beneath the steps Tom glimpses a small quantity of neatly stacked firewood. No smoke issues from the chimney.

Once he steers her through the front door she disengages herself and weaves a path down the hall toward the kitchen, removing the scarf and peeling off the gloves and letting them drop to the green-carpeted floor. Her fingertips graze the wall as she guides herself along.

"You'll stay for tea, of course."

"I should go. I have to move the car anyway."

"Oh, don't worry about that. Just make sure you remember for next time."

Tom closes the insulated door behind him, shutting out the cold. The hallway walls are painted eggshell and decorated with a few small paintings and photographs, some hanging straight, others just crooked enough that he notices. A set of shiny oak stairs leads up to a landing. It all has the look of recent construction.

He glances out at the Echo, which sits on the road where he left it, engine running. He's in the house of a drunken stranger who's left him to do as he pleases. He would be wise to leave this minute, before a situation that is merely odd cascades into the bizarre. But he is drawn to the cosy normalcy of his surroundings, the textures of unexceptional lives being lived. He has not been craving this, but now that he's here he can feel a crack in his heart being patched and filled, a wound he didn't even know he had suffered beginning to knit.

He hears a crash and a frightening clatter from the kitchen, removes his boots and hurries the length of the hallway. She is on her knees with her head in one of many open cupboards, rummaging through the clutter. A few steel cooking pots lie upended on the floor beside her.

"I can't find the teapot," she says, from the cupboard, her tone despairing. When she turns to him her eyes are brimming with tears.

"It doesn't matter," he says. He goes to her and, taking her under both arms, easily lifts her to her feet. She weighs almost nothing.

"I was going to make tea," she moans and wipes her face with her hand. Her voice is more like a little girl's than a grown woman's.

As he eases her across the floor and into a kitchen chair, he feels the line of her hip and buttocks hard against his thigh and wonders if she's doing it deliberately. Or maybe she's just off balance. One of her slippers is lying upside down on the floor, and the sight of her bare foot on the cold ceramic tile fills him with concern.

The kitchen is bright. He can finally get a good look at her. She's younger than he is, probably not yet forty. Her oval face is small and pale, the trembling bottom lip bitten and dry. She wears no rings. Her dark hair gleams and, when he allows his fingers to brush it, feels stiff and coarse.

His penis, dormant for months, begins to stir. He has to get out of here.

"Are you all right for now?"

"I made a mess of things. I always do."

"Do you want me to help you into the other room? Do you want to lie down?"

"Why aren't you nice to me?" she says, lifting one hand as if intending to slap him but instead striking out clumsily at air.

She slumps forward and he has to catch her to prevent her falling. She seems drunker than before. Words tumble from her mouth, getting in each other's way and losing their meaning. He wonders for a moment if there's a bottle hidden in the kitchen and arrives at the obvious answer: of course there is.

He lifts her into his arms and carries her to the living room. She emits a series of moans into his shoulder but when he lays her on the sofa her head falls to the side and her whole body goes limp. In a second she's snoring lightly.

Brushing the hair from her face, he stands over her, looking down. In sleep her features relax. The edges soften, the wrinkles melt away. There is something desperately childlike and fragile about her that clutches at his heart. He's momentarily reminded of Kathleen as she was when they first met, the skinny girl with the crooked smile. He's been with women since his marriage ended, but the act has always been ugly, impersonal, degrading. He hasn't felt this longing for intimacy and sharing, to be really close to someone, for years. He doesn't know her; has no idea who she is or what she's going through. Still, a part of him admires her for being brave enough to get drunk in the middle of the day. A part of him wants to join her.

Out of a silence that swells until it not only surrounds but inhabits him, emerges the ticking of a clock. He's holding his breath — has been holding it — for how long? He can't remember what his last breath felt like.

In the porch he pulls on his boots. He leaves the house. He must appear calm, normal, blameless. But at the bottom of the steps he stumbles and falls to his knees on the ground. His heart kicks against the cage of his chest.

TEN

HE SEES THEM — his family — as he's getting into another rental car in the parking lot behind the Quinpool Road shopping mall. From a hundred feet away he knows who it is. Automatically, as if his brain has switched itself off, he leaves his Wendy's fast-food breakfast on the front seat and follows them into the grocery store.

In the months immediately following his breakdown, during lucid moments, he could not escape them: reminders of Kathleen, Charlie, and Hannah were everywhere, in everything he saw, everything he touched, smelled, ate. His every thought turned back to them. To know that he could not be with them was an agony he took perverse delight in inflicting on himself. Once the medication kicked in his longing for them softened into a kind of nostalgia. He recalled mostly small moments — smiles and hugs — seemingly insignificant events that loomed large now they were all he had, but only rarely were these recollections accompanied by tears. Lately he thinks of them less often and recalls his ex-wife and children with the kind of tender fondness one reserves for a close friend who has long been absent. He has a single photograph each of Hannah and Charlie, but this morning he cannot remember the last time he drew them from his wallet.

He doesn't want to approach or speak to them. He's not prepared for an encounter. All he wants is to make sure they're okay. And he's not surprised either. He knew this was coming, that in the normal course of events it was inevitable that he would run into them somewhere. It's a wonder it hasn't happened before.

He grabs a cart and pushes it slowly along the produce aisle, keeping them in view but at a distance. He's not been in touch with Turcotte for ages, and so has no recent information, doesn't know how Charlie's recovery is going. Kathleen's hair is longer — otherwise she looks the same. Her face is calm, her eyes crinkle cheerfully when she smiles. She seems younger. He doesn't recognize the long beige jacket she's wearing. She places some lemons in a plastic bag, sorts through the onions and potatoes looking for the unblemished ones, a gesture — a manner — he knows intimately. Hannah and Charlie trail behind, singly, each absorbed in their own thoughts. Charlie is wearing a set of big black headphones that fit over his ears. The wire leads into his jacket pocket. Charlie's injured hand is wrapped in something white, a bandage maybe, but Tom's too far away to see clearly. Hannah selects a grapefruit from the pile and examines it. She's just playing. Tom knows she doesn't like grapefruit. She picks with her fingernail at something on the smooth yellow-green surface, then turns and shows what she's done to Charlie, who makes a face. Tom's amazed at how she's grown. He does a quick calculation and decides that two and a half years have passed. Charlie is ten and Hannah twelve.

He hears Kathleen telling Hannah to put the grapefruit back, and it's as if he's returning from a daydream. He swivels the cart abruptly in the other direction and with absurd intensity studies the display of loose carrots, chooses the biggest one and puts it in the cart. Lets them gain some ground. Suddenly he's aware of the piped-in music, an old song by Chris Isaac, "Blue Hotel." He used to have it on CD, but he'd left all that stuff behind. Gladly, he thought. He struggles for a moment with the tightness in his throat. Doggedly he gives the cart a shove, grabs a turnip and drops it next to the carrot.

They're making headway now, entering the bakery section while he lags behind in produce. Something that resembles anger exerts a mounting pressure behind his eyes.

He drifts toward the deli. There are enough people around that he feels safely obscured by the commotion and the swell of voices. He tosses a wedge of cheese into the cart. Kathleen is finished in the bakery and pushes her rapidly filling cart toward the meat section, which is around a corner. Tom follows, but at a casual pace. On the way he passes the fruit display and looks for the grapefruit that Hannah picked with her fingernail. Sure enough, the one on top has a fresh gouge in the skin. He places it in his cart, its value known only to him.

He dawdles, unsure how to proceed, and at the last moment before rounding the bend turns back. He really does want a loaf of bread. Whole wheat. This goes in with the carrot, turnip, cheese, and grapefruit. When he turns again toward the meat counter Kathleen and the kids are nowhere in sight. He wilts, but the shudder of disappointment is tempered by relief. Then someone moves out of the way and he spots them, further along than he thought they'd be. Kathleen swings the cart to the left and disappears down another aisle.

Now he has to be careful. He can't risk meeting them head on. He feels ridiculous as he creeps forward, trying not to get in anyone's way while keeping watch at the same time — clumsily legitimizing his presence beside the meat cooler by tossing a package of chicken drumsticks in with the pathetic assortment of items he's accumulated. He peeks down the aisle where he saw them go. At the far end Kathleen is speaking to Hannah and handing over some money — maybe to buy candy or gum. Charlie stands by, gazing around distractedly, not paying attention to anything. The headphones look uncomfortable, too big for his head. Tom pulls back. Unusual for Kathleen to be generous with treats at this time of the morning. Is it wise? But then, it's not his call. He looks again as Hannah takes the money and nods, her face solemn. Tom pushes his cart to the next aisle and waits. Hannah and Charlie walk by, toward the exit. He goes to the end of the aisle and sees them walking out of the store.

He takes a few more steps before slowing to a stop. He doesn't know what to do now. Does he really want to spend his morning following Kathleen from aisle to aisle, watching her fill her cart with groceries and then carry them out to the car? What would be the point? But then, what was the point of coming in here? Curiosity? To observe his children from a safe distance and then leave without speaking to them? To look for some sign that Kathleen is a neglectful mother?

He's asking himself these questions — taking a step forward, then back, when people excuse themselves to reach around him for items on the shelves — and does not see Kathleen approaching until she's almost upon him. In desperation he grabs a box from the shelf beside him and throws it into the cart. He's trying to turn the cart around when he hears, "Tom?"

He turns.

"It is you, then."

He's just staring at her. This moment has played itself in his head time and again, but now he doesn't know what to say.

"I'm glad to see you're eating well." She glances at his cart and raises her eyebrows, and he knows in an instant she's having him on, playing with him.

"Can I hug you?" he says finally. They step out from around their grocery carts and embrace lightly.

"I just happened to be here," he says, trying to explain. "I saw you and thought ... I don't know what I thought."

"He's not ready to see you yet, Tom," Kathleen says, turning away, her voice betraying a slight edge. But she recovers quickly and looks him straight in the eye. "He's not over the nightmares. It's going to be years. He might never be ready. You have to accept that."

Tom nods.

"What about Hannah?"

Kathleen shakes her head and Tom lowers his eyes to conceal a spasm of annoyance.

"Not to see her, but just … how is she?"

"She's coping. We're all coping. It's not been easy. I appreciate you letting us be and sticking with your medications. I know it hasn't been easy for you either. We've both seen enough of this to know how destructive it can be."

Tom nods briefly, feeling a stab of guilt because he's been putting off visiting his mother. "How's your Dad?"

"Oh, doing well. Out at the cottage."

The silence stretches. He's afraid to ask about her sister, Abby, who, for all he knows, might be dead. Is this really all they have to say to each other after two and a half years?

"I'm sorry I had to rush the divorce. I didn't see any other way to move on."

Tom nods again.

"Do you ever hear from your father, or Beverly?"

"No. Not a word."

"I'm sorry."

Tom shrugs. He is desperate, now that it's nearing its end, for her not to regret this encounter.

"Are you still weaving?"

Kathleen smiles and the warmth of relief spreads through him.

"It's my business now, Tom. It's what I do. After everything that happened ... I just felt, you know, why not? It's what I love. Dad helped me get started, but it's doing well. I can't describe the feeling."

Out of pride Tom wants to hold her, but instead takes a step back.

"What about Charlie's —" As he struggles to find the word he lifts his left hand and flexes it. "Movement. Mobility?" He appeals to her with his eyes. "Has he recovered, you know, some of the use?"

Kathleen's eyes narrow slightly. The smile is gone.

"He's tried. He lost the middle finger. There was damage to the nerves. But you know all this." She looks into his face. "He still cries in the night." She leaves this hanging for a moment before going on. "They tell me I shouldn't, but I go to him. I can't bear for him to be alone with his pain."

There are tears in her eyes now. But she doesn't look away.

"You know if I could do anything to take it back —"

"I know, I know. It wasn't your fault. And I'm not saying it was. But still, I can't just —"

He wants to ask if there's any chance of seeing her again, to stay in touch. But she's wiping her eyes, wrapping it up.

"It was good to see you, Tom. You're looking well."

"I'm glad I followed you," he says, half in jest because he only half believes it.

"I should go. I sent the kids over to the Wendy's to get breakfast burgers, or pancakes. Something. There's no end to what they make now for kids to eat." She forces a smile.

He doesn't know what to say. "Good-bye, then," is what comes out of his mouth.

"Good-bye, Tom."

She pushes her cart past his and a moment later he resumes pushing his own. He retraces his route, returning his selections to their places in the displays where he found them, except for the bread and the grapefruit. It's slow going because he's moving against the flow. Fifteen minutes have passed by the time he's done, long enough by his estimation for her to have completed her shopping and left the store.

When Tom gets back to the car, his breakfast — an egg and ham muffin, hash browns, and coffee — is bone cold. He eats it anyway. For the next five minutes no one goes in or comes out of Wendy's. He imagines Kathleen watching him through the restaurant window, keeping the kids in their seats with one excuse after another, waiting for him to drive off. He wonders if she's involved with anyone, but there's no way for him to know. He couldn't have asked because it's none of his business and it would only have pissed her off. Part of him doesn't care; part of him cares deeply. Both are dangerous. How will he ever learn to steer between the two?

Twenty minutes later there's no sign of them. He starts the car, waits a moment longer. Then, with no destination in mind, he drives off.

ELEVEN

IT TAKES HIS MOTHER three long years to die. By the time her heart gives out she has been bedridden for more than a year, huddled beneath over-starched hospital sheets, her eyelids occasionally opening into slits through which nothing seems to pass. Tom had seen her very infrequently before his diagnosis, and of course didn't see her at all for the year he was in the Abbie J. Lane. Even on his release he put off visiting, but after his encounter with the drunk lady he started again. The two women have become inextricably linked in his mind. He supposes this is because of the impulse he felt to try to help the drunk woman find a way through whatever dark night of the soul had eclipsed the part of her that knew how to cope. He often thought of going back out there. This time she would be sober and lucid, and in his fantasy they would sit down and talk their way through her problems. But after a few months of not acting on the impulse, he found it increasingly difficult to recall what she looked like and began to wonder why he'd imagined she would open her door to him a second time, and even if she did, how he could help anyone with anything when some days it took all his strength just to get out of bed. And it was then that he realized his mother was also struggling through darkness, and while he couldn't do anything for the stranger who had taken him into her home, he could at least try to help the woman he had neglected for years.

On that first visit he found very little had changed. She was in the same ward, and facing the same television in the common room. Even a few of the other inmates looked familiar. Her skin had puckered and yellowed, like paper exposed too long to moisture, and her eyes seemed to have receded into her skull, as if she'd withdrawn even further from a world she had rejected years ago. The tiny purple veins trembling beneath the skin of her forehead and temples made him think of something embryonic. She had lost flesh: her wrists were as delicate as a child's. Her hair had gone completely grey. The last time he'd visited she had been creeping about on her own, using a toehold on reality to navigate her surroundings. Now she sat slumped in a wheelchair, her eyes vacant, her mouth slack — one of the droolers. A nurse explained that thirty years of anti-psychotic treatments had caused her body tissue to start breaking down. Her muscles had atrophied. Her mind was gone. It was a natural part of the process, for someone in her condition.

Tom nodded, recognizing in his docile acceptance of these pronouncements an unappealing mannerism of his father's for which he'd never had any patience. But what could he do except take what he was offered and remain silent on the subject of his own medications?

He forced himself to stay and, later, to return.

At first he could hardly make himself look at her without shrinking in revulsion. She emitted a pungent feral smell, medicinal yet grossly human. Every now and then she released a breathy sigh, which he attributed to gastrointestinal functions rather than any effort to communicate. But as weeks and then months went by he attained a kind of peace with what she had become and even developed a deep admiration for the utter simplicity of her existence, the fact that nothing in the world could approach her or have the least impact upon her serenity. She possessed an enviable immunity from the pain, sorrow, and calamity of daily living. She had been spared the dissolution of her family, her husband's descent into alcoholism, her daughter's drug use, her son's psychotic collapse. Who wouldn't prefer oblivion to bearing witness to that kind of failure?

Tom wheeled her from room to room. It was exercise for him, a change of scene for her. On fine days he took her outside and parked her chair at one of the vantage points overlooking the harbour. Tom smoked a cigarette and gazed down at the bustling harbour traffic, or up at the sea birds hovering high above the water, and tried not to think about what he was doing — did not ask himself why he was spending time with a woman who — was it thirty years ago? — had abandoned him to a future of isolation and loss. He was not seeking reparation or revenge, or an apology. He did not feel hard done by. Mostly, in her company, he felt content — and, to a limited degree, safe — as if the simplicity with which she passed the hours was something he could share and perhaps even absorb for as long as they were together.

At mealtimes he wheeled her into the cafeteria and fed her the daily soup or mashed potatoes or green jello. She ate with the distracted willingness of an infant, and it was only then that he allowed himself to consider the person inhabiting her skin, to imagine that at one time she had watched with great satisfaction while her family enjoyed a meal she had prepared, and that she had entertained expectations of a full life and hopes for her children.

He was at work when she had her stroke, and he got the message on his cell phone. From then on he visited her in the medical ward. He spent hours in her small private room, reading aloud from books like *Oliver Twist* and *To Kill a Mockingbird* and *All Quiet on the Western Front* — books he was supposed to have read in school but hadn't because he was too distracted or busy, or just couldn't be bothered. Now, against his expectations, he was gripped by these stories of poverty and racial injustice and the dehumanization of war. His mother lay still beneath the sheets, her body drawing nourishment from the IV tube in her arm and expelling a trickle of urine into a bag hanging from the bed frame. The only sounds were the soft whistle of her breathing and the intermittent rustle of a page being turned. Often as he sat there he thought back to his childhood, before Beverly was born, trying to remember. Had he been happy? Probably. How do you know for sure when you're young and don't know anything else? In his mind he heard his mother laughing, saw his father smile. Those things had happened. How could they not have? He had no memory of being particularly unhappy. But that whole part of his life was shrouded in a kind of mist and only partly visible, like something you glimpse in vague outline through frosted glass. What came after was so much more vivid.

He was not there when she died. It happened in the middle of the week, just before daybreak. Once again he got the message on his cell, but this time he did not leave work until the end of his shift. She had already been dead for several hours when he checked his phone. There was no reason to hurry.

She had not been present in his life, but he felt touched nonetheless by a jagged edge of loss. He wasn't about to cry, but the feeling of emptiness was nearly overwhelming.

Instead of walking straight home he went to the Smitty's down the street for breakfast and sat alone in a booth. The waitress brought his coffee and called him "dear" when she took his order. He sipped the coffee and listened to the chatter of the other customers and thought it was good to be among people.

TWELVE

TOM, ALONE IN THE TINY CHAPEL, glances at his watch. The service is scheduled to begin in ten minutes. A tinny stream of organ music oozes tremulously from invisible speakers. The windowless room is too bright, but the fluorescent lights can't be dimmed. Plastic lilies leaning in tall slim vases have a gloomy air of neglect about them. Nothing about the faded gold-and-white-striped wallpaper or the twenty-five empty folding chairs arranged in rows on the well-trodden green carpet is uplifting. But space in any funeral home is hard to come by at short notice.

The sleek metal urn containing his mother's ashes sits on a small table at the head of the room. There is no photograph because he was unable to find one. He feels ill at ease in a suit and tie, his thinning hair combed and slicked. His hands and feet seem to him disproportionately large – large enough to frighten children. His shoes, purchased nearly new the day before, are scuffed and, he realized an hour ago, too tight. He's afraid he smells of something other than aftershave and

antiperspirant – sweat and the solvents from his cleaning job
that cling to his skin no matter how long he showers or how
vigorously he scrubs.

After his mother's death he wasn't sure how to carry out
his obligations. He was asked what her wishes were regarding
burial but didn't know, so when the funeral home suggested
cremation he saw no reason to object. Had his mother been
at all religious? Should he hire a priest? Rent a church hall?
Should there be flowers? If so, what kind? His ignorance
seemed to have no bounds.

He wanders out of the room, up the hallway to the water
fountain. His hands are greasy with sweat. He needs a cigarette badly. What initially seemed like a good idea now strikes
him as exactly the kind of blundering miscalculation he would
commit. What if nobody shows up? What if, after all, his
mother exited this world without leaving traces of herself in
anyone's memory but his own? But someone has to remember
her. He has done his best to get the word out. He placed the
sketchy and uninformative obituary not just in the Halifax
papers, but also in the New Minas paper. Then, recalling that
she had once spoken about growing up in Winnipeg, he phoned
the obituary in to the *Free Press* as well. He wanted Kathleen
to know, and through her, Charlie and Hannah, but when
he phoned the lawyer's number a woman informed him in
brusque tones that Turcotte was no longer with the firm, had
left no contact information, and – to his further inquiry –
that they had no Kathleen Brackett (or Kathleen Merriam)

on file as a client. She was not listed in the phone book. He thought of driving to the house, but in the end dropped a letter in the mail.

A week after his mother died a nurse phoned to ask when he would be collecting her things, which turned out to be a wedding ring, a social insurance card and a dozen or so photographs of himself and Beverly as children. From the moment it slipped out of the manila envelope, the ring has been in his pocket. He keeps pulling it out and examining it. It is a plain, unmarked gold band. He has no memory of ever seeing it on his mother's finger.

A service is taking place in another chapel in the funeral home. A few men in dark suits linger in the hallway, speaking in undertones. One of them turns a stricken glance in his direction. Tom bows his head and retreats. Resumes his seat. Waits.

Finally there is a sound of shuffling. A little lady in a blue coat enters and takes a seat at the very rear. Tom observes her with a sidelong glance as she arranges herself in the chair, rests her purse primly in her lap and gazes expectantly around the room. Their eyes meet and she gives him a tentative smile, then looks away. Her smallness is almost cartoonish, and she wears her greying hair piled on top of her head beneath a black hat.

He has no idea who she is, and is preparing to speak to her when a funeral home attendant signals to him from the hallway. Tom looks at his watch. It's almost time.

Three women arrive. He recognizes them from the hospital. They are nurses who work in the ward where his mother stayed. He greets them and shakes hands with each. He should know their names and is embarrassed that he has to ask: Joan, Cindy, and Rita.

"Thanks for coming," he says. After not speaking for more than an hour his voice cracks.

Rita, the oldest of the three, grips his hand. Her eyes fill with tears.

"Rebecca was such a good patient," she manages before her face contorts and the tears start flowing for real. Cindy and Joan exchange a look while Cindy passes her a tissue. With the tissue pressed to her face Rita whispers, "I'm sorry. I didn't want this to happen."

A twinge of panic jabs him in the gut as, with gentle firmness, he extracts his hand from her grip. Suddenly his bladder feels about to burst. The lady in the blue coat sits waiting for the service to begin. Again he tries to place her and fails. He feels like running out to the street, running until he can't run any further. He sees himself doing this, leaving everything behind, himself included − all the things he's done, all the damage he's caused − running until he's so far away nothing is familiar and he's in a place where nothing can touch him.

Then, with a clatter, the attendant is shutting the doors. The organ music is silenced mid phrase.

Tom stands beside the table where the urn is sitting and introduces himself. He clears his throat. Rita sniffles loudly, looks down and dabs her eyes with the tissue. He does not try to hide his discomfort, which will be obvious no matter what he does. The collar of his shirt chafes his neck, his face is burning, he's itching from head to toe. But he is determined to see this through.

"I didn't know my mother very well," he says, looking at the floor. He shakes his head. The admission strikes him as pathetic. But what can he do? It's the truth. "She wasn't there much after I turned ten. It was only later that I found out what happened, that it wasn't her choice. Now I know that she would've been there for Bev and me if she could've. But whatever it was that was in her head took her right away from us. Being where I been, I know you can't control the like of that. It's just the way things work out." He lifts his gaze and scans the room, avoiding the eight female eyes turned toward him. "I'm not complaining. I can't worry about stuff that's over and done with. I don't feel like anybody owes me or anything like that. I just wish I could've got to know her better." He pauses as a glimpse of a life that could have been flashes before his eyes: a family outing — him, his parents, and Beverly — the four of them taking a drive. A deer is feeding in the brush by the side of the road. He calls out and points. Everyone looks. He remembers the car: his father's decrepit Mercury, green and pocked with rust. This can't be a memory. Nothing about it is right. But even if it is only wish fulfilment he doesn't want to let it go. It's a sunny day, they're heading for the beach. His father switches on the radio and the car fills with the sound of Willie Nelson singing "Seasons of my Heart." This is what families do, he thinks. The vision fades and there he is, standing in the smallest chapel of the Atlantic Funeral Home on Bayers Road, in front of twenty-one empty chairs.

Rita blows her nose. She smiles encouragingly at him, but her eyes are red. It disturbs him to think that this woman can weep at his mother's passing while he cannot, that the drugs have flattened his emotions so that he can't even stake a claim to a grief that's rightfully his. The terrible calm that engulfs him is massive and implacable, like a smooth sea stretching toward a still horizon. Like a fogbound island. Like a huge, hovering sky. But however inappropriate the calm is, it's the best he can manage. He hopes his mother would understand.

"I have some good memories. She wasn't always like how she was in the hospital. She took me to movies sometimes when I was small. We went to the lunch counter at Zellers and I got a chocolate milkshake. That was my favourite. Nobody makes milkshakes like that anymore. I guess in the end that's all you can hope for, these things you remember."

He sputters to a halt, running out of words the way a car runs out of fuel, and ends with a shrug.

"Thanks for coming today. I can't say nothing more than that."

He lowers his eyes, marches up the aisle between the rows of chairs to the rear of the chapel and opens the doors. He feels like he can breathe again.

The nurses are standing. Rita dabs at her eyes. He accompanies them into the lobby, where they exchange some pleasantries and he sees them out the door.

He returns to the chapel. The lady in the blue coat is standing beside the table, staring down at the urn. Tom studies her, but she remains a mystery.

He clears his throat.

"Sorry for not saying anything before," he says, watching her turn. "I was too nervous, I guess."

"You don't recognize me, do you?" Holding her purse by the strap with both hands, she smiles as if confounding him constitutes some sort of victory. "But why should you? It's been a long time. More than thirty years. I hardly recognize myself after all this time."

She speaks in a soft, slightly gravelly voice and with the precise enunciation of a teacher. Tom shakes his head.

"I'm sorry, I don't —"

"We lived next door to you in Black River. I'm Delia Joffrey. Rebecca — your mother — was my best friend for a time."

They come back to him with sudden, wrenching clarity: those years in Black River, the house shielded from the highway by a patch of land covered by a scattering of birch and spruce trees. The smells of baking, on wet days the swish of car tires on asphalt, the pond that froze over in winter.

"You had a daughter. We went to school together." But beyond long wavy brown hair and glasses he recalls nothing, though at one time he considered her a friend. Maybe she wore knee socks and black shoes. Maybe she smelled like sunshine.

"Hallie. Yes. She's in Calgary. Married her high school sweetheart."

"That's great." Tom glances at the floor. "Uh, I wish I remembered more. It's all a bit hazy."

Mrs. Joffrey approaches him between the rows of empty chairs. "I'm not surprised. You were very young." She cocks her head and stares with a boldness he finds unnerving. He does not look away, and for a moment it seems she is about to make a comment, but in the end she says nothing. Her eyes are blue, her skin tone pale and faintly yellow, as if some illness has recently left its mark on her. She must be seventy and yet her complexion is clear, her skin unwrinkled. "I'm sorry," she says, opening her purse. "I'm dying for a smoke."

"I DIDN'T KNOW what happened exactly. There's no doubt in my mind she was happy about the baby. I seem to remember something about money problems. But she was too proud to ask for help. It was just a feeling, I suppose. Her clothes and her hair: she always looked a bit worn down."

"Doesn't surprise me. I always figured we were living close to the bone. There was always enough, but never much to spare. We ate leftovers a lot. Mom knew how to make it last. I think Dad had trouble finding steady work."

"He was an odd one, your Dad. He didn't talk much, at least not to me. Had his ways, I guess you would say. Maybe he was just shy, but I thought he was strange. No offence. Harold, bless his soul, got more out of him than I ever did. Said Charlie was a real joker — but I suppose you had to be able to appreciate his sense of humour. Guess it was a taste I never developed. But Rebecca loved him. That's one thing I'm sure of."

Tom raises the cigarette to his lips and pulls in the smoke. They are standing side by side in the paved parking lot behind the funeral home, outside the rear entrance. It is cool for April. Above them the sun struggles but fails to find a chink in the steely cloud cover suspended over the city like a helmet. Mrs. Joffrey has smoked two cigarettes for his one, each time mercilessly grinding the spent butt beneath the broad heel of her sensible shoe. A few people from the other service gradually disperse in cars or on foot.

"But after Beverly was born, nothing was ever really the same. We got together a few times, but I could tell something wasn't right. And then your mother kind of disappeared. And after that spell in the hospital it was like some stranger had taken her place. She wasn't rude or anything, but when I was in the house she kept looking at me like she didn't know why I was there or like she thought maybe I was waiting for a chance to steal something. I could tell she didn't want me around. She started coming up with excuses for not letting me in. Left me standing out there in the rain more than once. Then she just stopped answering the door and the phone. I'm sorry to say I gave up. I sent Harold over to talk to your Dad because I was worried, but as far as I know nothing came of it. He seemed to take what we were trying to do personally, like maybe he thought we were blaming him. Told Harold we were meddling where it was none of our business. But really, it wasn't like that. We just wanted to help."

"Well, I appreciate that. Thanks." Tom drops the cigarette and crushes it with his foot. His stomach lurches and there's a spasm of discomfort, but he doesn't feel hungry or ill. It's just the tension of the day: the weirdness of putting on a public face. And hearing about the past, which he craves and detests.

"Is your father living?"

"I don't know." It's almost a shock to hear himself admit it. How can he not know if his father is alive or dead? What must she think of him? "I was hoping maybe he'd show up if he was around. The same with Bev. I thought if she saw something in the paper it would get to her and she'd come. But I didn't hear from them. So I guess it means they're either dead or living somewhere else."

"Oh, Tom." She reaches out and touches his hand. "You did good today, putting this together. Rebecca would have been pleased."

His mind races with questions, but he resists asking and prolonging the conversation. More than anything he wants to be alone. In a few minutes she has ground out her third and last cigarette, wished him well, and is striding purposefully across the parking lot to the street. He watches the tiny figure in the blue coat until she is out of sight.

For now he will leave his mother's ashes in the funeral home vault. Someday he will decide what to do with them. He had thought he might discuss it with Kathleen, but there has been no word from her. A shudder of disappointment clenches his chest and causes tightness in his throat, and it is only now that he realizes how anxiously he had hoped that Kathleen would show up today with the children. Was it an unreasonable hope? Perhaps. But then too quickly the disappointment fades. Like some flickering memory, it eludes his grasp after a brief moment of blinding clarity. He reaches for it, but it is no longer there. And this becomes the source of a new disappointment that, seconds later, melts away to nothing. Equilibrium returns. Alone, he finishes a last cigarette. There is not another person in sight.

In a short while he has concluded his business at the funeral home and is climbing into his rental car.

THIRTEEN

IN A RECURRING DREAM the phone rings. The voice at the other end is unfamiliar. It belongs to a young man.

"Dad?"

Sometimes the caller is Kathleen. She's asking him to come to the house to fix something, and, by the way, he may as well stay for dinner.

He goes to work. Comes home. The routine is a solace and only occasionally seems like confinement.

He goes to work. Comes home. It's six in the morning, dark out, raining. What was he thinking a minute ago?

His mother has been dead for eight months. He has been living temporarily in this apartment for three years, going on four.

FOURTEEN

TOM CAN'T SLEEP. He sits on the corner of the bed, which in daylight folds into a sofa. Aware of his bare feet resting on the cool wooden floor, he draws a hand slowly across his face. The coarseness of his whiskers is another reminder that he is alive, that — unavoidably — he is his father's son. For the hundredth time the notion flits across his consciousness that his father is gone, and for a brief moment he finds himself wondering where — before the thought dissolves, expunged by weariness, swallowed up by the dark core of his mind. He cannot recall a time when this bone-weariness did not inhabit him: carving a hollow space in his head and making his limbs feel like rubber. He has abandoned reading because he can't follow long sequences of words. He can no longer drive a car because his attention wanders and he loses the thread of what he's doing. But when he lies down and switches off the light, his eyes refuse to close and his mind whirls. There are always sounds from the street: conversations, sirens, empty cans being kicked, car horns, the pulsating bass of a car stereo.

The whispering voice — the unceasing conversation — flows from the other apartment, crosses the landing and seeps under the door. The glare from the school's security lights floods the room, exposing as ruthlessly as daylight the threadbare furnishings, the dents in the walls, and the uneven floorboards.

Idly, he lines up the nine pill bottles side by side across the coffee table. They stand like chess pieces or sentinels guarding an entryway, each wearing a white or yellow or brown uniform and white cap. A few are fat and squat, a couple are slender and taller than the rest. Each throws a distinctive shadow. They are his only friends, his intimate confidants. He knows them by name, by colour, by shape: round white olanzapine, the red capsule risperidone, the pale blue lozenge clomipramine. They have saved him and they are killing him. He's been warned about side-effects and understands the signs: the trembling, the blanks in his memory, the bewildered fumbling for words, the sensation of drowning that wrenches him awake night after night. The doctors have reduced the dosages, adjusted the cocktail. Nothing changes.

He feels like a spectator watching a drama unfold. Who is this man whose paranoid delusions and violent outbursts have driven his family away, isolating him with the horrible efficiency of a deadly and contagious illness? Why can he do nothing to save himself? Who is this creature who struggles every day to maintain a grip on the remnants of who he was, who can't remember what led him into this blind alley?

But then rage rumbles into wakefulness, lifts its head and peers blindly into the dark. Tom looks on as his arm extends, his hand opens, the limb quivers. He clenches his muscles, steeling them for the battle that is to come. His fist is suspended above the line of bottles. He will sweep them off the table to the floor. He will pour their contents into the toilet and flush them away. Why has it taken so long for him to realize that only by destroying the pills and breaking free of his dependence will he be able to live a normal life? Once the pills are gone there can be no doubt that he will win back what he has lost, because it is the pills, not the illness, that have turned him into the stranger who forgets his own name and can't control the twitching of his limbs. And the stranger is responsible for the nightmare his life has become.

Free of the pills, he will walk the streets as a complete human being, someone who belongs among others and doesn't frighten people away with a gloomy, hulking presence. He will set out along Agricola Street, past the Commons and the Citadel, crossing Sackville Street and strolling toward Spring Garden Road like anyone else. This is the freedom he deserves. It's within his grasp.

And then comes the fading. The resolve that only seconds before gripped his brain with a vivid pulsing intensity, propelling him toward action — this resolve slips back into the shadowy recess of his mind, grows soft, formless, melts, and dissolves. His anger nods, falls into a doze, resumes its slumber. Perplexed, he gazes at his clenched fist, relaxes and uncurls his fingers, lowers his hand.

He notices the bottles of pills scattered across the coffee table. Strange. Why would he do that? He picks one up and reads the label: aripiprazole. This is the latest, the most recent addition. It is supposed to reduce anxiety and ease his transition from the old regimen. But the others are still important. He can't mess with them. They are the only things keeping him alive.

Carefully he gathers the bottles and returns them to the cabinet in the bathroom. The meds schedule is printed in bold black letters and taped to the wall beside the mirror as a reminder because lately he's liable to forget, and forgetting will upset the intricate balance his doctors have achieved through years of trial and error.

He feels strange, a bit dizzy. He sits on the closed toilet. He just needs to rest for a minute.

His mother. Her image leaps into his mind. His body tenses. He's on his feet. He can't keep putting it off. He's forgotten to visit her. He has to go see her. Today. He'll do it today.

Then he remembers. He slumps forward. Sits back down. His breathing slows.

He gets up and closes the cabinet. From the mirror, from an ashen face sunk in shadow, eyes peer out at him. He hardly recognizes them. Over the last few months his hair has thinned and his gums have grown tender and started bleeding. A couple of his teeth are loose. He's exhausted and nauseated, but relief is on the way. New drugs being tested will make him feel much better. That's what the doctor said.

He wipes a stream of spittle from the corner of his lip.

In the other room he drags a chair over to the window. The light rain that fell overnight has resolved into a persistent mist. The street is slick; headlights of passing cars throw dazzling reflections against the wet asphalt. Across the street a homeless man huddles in the recess of a doorway, head bent, motionless. A light wind tosses grocery bags and two empty plastic water bottles around on the pavement in a jittery ballet. Tom raises the window to let in some air. It's December and cold but not frigid. The damp air smells of metal and decay and the sodden last days of autumn. He lights a cigarette and settles in to watch the morning's procession of vehicles and pedestrians.

He is lucky to be alive. So lucky. It could have turned out differently.

ACKNOWLEDGEMENTS

Perfect World took shape over several years as I worked on other projects, starting as a short story and growing longer as I filled out Tom's story and became better acquainted with the problems he was facing. After completing a first draft, I sent the manuscript to Richard Cumyn, whose advice was forthright and valuable, especially with regard to the ending. In 2014 I shared a later draft with Chris Bucci at The McDermid Agency and finally with Kelsey Attard, Debbie Willis, Anna Boyar, and Barbara Scott at Freehand Books. Their positive responses and numerous suggestions have helped see the project through to this final stage.

Thanks to Enitharmon Press for permission to quote from Phoebe Hesketh's poem "A Very Small Casualty," which appears in her collection *Netting the Sun.*

As always, my wife Collette has sustained me through the writing of this book. Her love and support make everything possible.

I have attempted a truthful portrait of someone who, through no fault of his own, loses control of his world and can only watch as it falls to pieces around him. No one should have to experience what Tom Brackett goes through in these pages, but the fact is that people of all ages and in every walk of life face similar struggles every day. I do not mean to trivialize these struggles by depicting them in a work of fiction.

IAN COLFORD's work has appeared in Canadian literary publications from coast to coast. His first book, *Evidence* (Porcupine's Quill, 2008), received the Margaret and John Savage First Book Award at the Atlantic Book Awards. It was also shortlisted for the Danuta Gleed Literary Award, the Thomas Head Raddall Atlantic Fiction Award, and the ReLit Award. His second book, *The Crimes of Hector Tomás* (Freehand Books, 2012), won Trade Book of the Year at the 2013 Alberta Book Awards. Ian works at Dalhousie University and lives with his wife Collette in Halifax.

This book was typeset in FF Tundra by Ludwig Übele and Mostra Nuova by Mark Simonson Studio.